W9-CNN-465

Spencer Road ❧

Spencer Road ～

A Short Story Sequence

Morris Smith

The University of Tennessee Press
Knoxville

Earlier verisons of "Spencer Road" and "Bird" were in *descant* and *Ellipsis*, respectively.
"Division" appeared in *The Snake Nation Review* 12 (Spring/Summer 1997). Some
material is reprinted, by permission, from Sam Heys and Allen B. Goodwin, *The
Winecoff Fire* (Atlanta: Longstreet Press, 1993).

The paper in this book meets the minimum requirements of the American National
Standard for Permanence of Paper for Printed Library Materials. The binding materials
have been chosen for strength and durability. Printed on recycled paper.

Library of Congress Cataloging-in-Publication Data

Smith, Morris, 1928–
Spencer Road : a short story sequence / Morris Smith.— 1st ed.
    p. cm.
ISBN 0-87049-995-5 (cloth: alk. paper)
    I. Title.
PS3569.M537835S65 1997
813'.54—dc21   97-21056

For Sister and Sonny

Contents

Spencer Road ∼

The road is different now from back then, years ago, when Bird walked its white ruts. She lived up near the start, where the dirt road branched off the highway—the hardroad, she used to say—and twice a day she'd walk from her house to ours, where Spencer Road ended. Mainly she kept to the packed-down tire tracks; but if a car happened by, she would move toward the ditch where the ground was soft and gray. Turning, she'd stare at the car with curious, amused eyes. She liked to see who it was, driving down our road. If she knew the riders—black or white—she'd throw up her hand.

When we, the Spencer children, were playing outside, we'd see Bird round the curve, still quite a ways from our house. The road broke away from the woods there and hugged a grassy oak grove. We'd wave, watching her come, as sure as time, scuffing along the dirt surface in her men's tennis shoes that she'd take off as soon as she stepped into the kitchen. Then she'd pad around the wooden floor in wide brown feet that turned flaky gray along the outside edges. Bird was on the tall side, her face thin and shy, and on one shoulder a growth the size of a small eggplant, that she called a goiter, ballooned out, pushing against the sleeve of her dress. Her hair was covered with a puffy white cap that she wore winter and summer.

Sometimes we would cut across the oak grove to meet her. "Well, I've bumped up the road one more time," she'd say, and hand us the round tin pan she brought empty to our house; when she left at dark, it'd be full. Fighting to see who would carry her pan, we would trail her down the path through the grove, across the wooden stile by the pump house, and into the back yard.

"Frank, she's been drinking again," Mother said to my father, who sat reading the Sunday *Atlanta Journal*, feet propped on the woodbox. "I smelled liquor on her breath this morning, and she was practically reeling when she cleared the table just now." Mother sounded as though she'd been saving this for the right moment, when everybody was together and still.

It was summer. We were back from church, had eaten dinner, and Gilbert, Maggie, and I were sitting on the living room rug with the brightly colored funnies spread out, "The Katzenjammer Kids" at the top of one page. Gilbert was eleven, I was eight, and Maggie only five. We looked up to see how serious this was going to be. Papa lowered his paper.

"It's this way every other Sunday now," Mother went on, keeping her voice low. She stood in front of the cold fireplace in a blue voile Sunday dress, pearls at her neck. Her hands were clasped behind her, the way she would have held them if a fire were burning and she was warming them. Suddenly Mother turned, her brown eyes behind her rimless glasses looking hard at me. "Elizabeth, you noticed her. Didn't you laugh when she tried to take your plate? You weren't finished."

"No, ma'am," I said, wishing I'd kept my mouth shut when I found myself without a plate, my fork in mid-air. "I was finished. I was laughing at Gil."

"I doubt that." Mother lifted her chin. "Well, my patience is coming to an end."

Gil and I glanced at each other. A few months before, her patience *had* come to an end. That Sunday, she'd actually walked through the swinging door to the kitchen and fired Bird—told her to get her pan and leave, not even to finish with dinner, not to lock the door to the kitchen as Bird always did on the way out. Then Mother, her lips tight, marched back into the living room where the three of us children were sitting on the piano bench—lined up like the three "see-no-evil" monkeys. Papa began to talk easy, but Mother just sat in an armchair and shook her head. Maggie began to wail. None of us moved from the piano bench, but the crying spread when Bird tiptoed in from the kitchen, head tucked so you saw only the top of her white cap. She asked Mother to give her another chance. Mother fussed— said Bird ought to be ashamed and asked her to promise she'd stop drinking. Then it was all over.

This time it seemed that things wouldn't go that far. Papa said he'd talk to Bird and folded his newspaper. "I'll give her money to Gus on Saturdays, or maybe to Mizell," he added, and started for the kitchen.

"Bird says Mizell's going to De-troit," chirped Maggie, turning the funny-paper to "Jiggs." Mizell was Bird's son and sometimes he'd sit in the kitchen, waiting for his mother. Maggie liked him because he'd lift her and let her ride piggy-back.

"Say Detroit, not Dee-troit," corrected Mother. She sounded less cross.

It was Saturday. An orange road-scraper, its long blade crusted with dirt, sat like a huge praying mantis in the clearing across from the front yard. Every few months the scraper would creep down our road, gears screeching, engine sounding like a train, as the metal blade leveled the ruts and washboard bumps. Sometimes the crew would leave it for the night—there on the far side of the rounded dirt clearing, the place where the road ended. Then they would come back early the next day. This was the first time they'd left it over a weekend. When I woke up at six that morning and saw the road-scraper still there, I couldn't wait to tell Gil. For once I'd spotted something before him.

"I'm going to climb to the top of that thing," bragged Gil at breakfast after Mother and Papa had left the table. Bird was collecting the dishes.

"Better watch out," she said, stopping by Gil's chair. "Scraper nearly got me yestiddy evening. Heading home 'bout dark, I saw it rambling up the road with that big blade stretched out—wider than ever. Had to jump clean pass the ditch to keep from having the ground cut out from under me." Bird laughed low, putting the back of her hand to her mouth to cover her bad teeth. To her, everything had a funny side to it, except when Mother fired her. Sometimes she got in a fit of muffled laughter, her eyes watering, when somebody did something dumb in the kitchen, like stumbling on the doorstep or spilling peas.

"It's not going to cut the ground from under me." Gil walled his big brown eyes. He had a peppy expression, kind of like Mickey Mouse. "I'm going to drive it."

"You mean, play-like," said Bird. "Playing driving ain't doing it." She lifted the corner of her mouth and gave him a "you're-still-not-so-big" smile. "Mind out, climbing on that thing. If you fall on a blade, it'll cut."

Gil promised to be careful, and Bird patted his shoulder. Gilbert was her favorite—maybe because he was a boy and looked like Papa. Bird was older than Papa, but they had played together growing up. When they talked about those times, one would start telling a story and the other would finish up.

"Who's going to cook for Mizell in De-troit?" Maggie chimed in. She dipped her toast in the flowered cup Mother had left on the table and brought the bread up brown and dripping. Coffee-toast, she called it.

"That's God's business, and his. He say he's leaving next week." Bird reached for Gil's egg-smeared plate. "You quit slopping coffee on the tablecloth, Maggie."

"And who's Papa going to give your money to so you won't buy whis-key?" asked Maggie, dividing the word just the way Mother did.

"Mind your own business," snapped Gil.

"Yeah! Hush about whiskey," I said, talking loud for me. How awful it would be if Bird really got fired. Without her, the house would seem empty; we'd just rattle from room to room. I vowed never to laugh again if she picked up my plate too soon.

Gil ran to the sliding wooden doors to the living room, shoved them open, and turned. "Come on, Elizabeth."

❧

The morning was hot. Sun poured down on the clearing, a bright island surrounded by slim young oaks, and in the center sat the road-scraper. The orange metal glowed. Across the front, a silver blade stretched out wider than the tires, and three smaller blades trailed from the back like short shiny tails. The scraper made me think of a dragon, a mechanical dragon, but somehow like those in the stories about knights in our *Book House for Children* set.

I stopped under a tree. Gil swung up on a huge tire and climbed all the way to the cab, where a faded purple umbrella shaded the driver's seat. He spun the steering wheel, puffed out his cheeks, and made screeching noises, pretending he was driving. In a minute I joined him. We touched all the switches without turning anything on, then crawled way out on a skinny arm, bent like a giant elbow, and hopped from one section of warm orange metal to the next.

Back on the ground, we laughed at our funny faces in the gleaming front blade. Whitish dirt caked on the lower edge made lacy collars below our long pointed chins. Gil touched the silver metal and quickly pulled back his hand. "That blade is hot as hell."

Maggie, in a pink-checked sunsuit, was walking from the house, and she shook her head so hard that her sandy hair swung. She had a Dutch-boy cut, same as me, but my hair was darker—by two shades, Mother said. "Gil," she called, "you better not let Mother hear you say hell."

❧

On Saturday afternoons after dinner, Bird scoured the kitchen floor and left around three. She didn't come back to cook supper.

The kitchen was big with the stove in the middle, sitting on a piece of dark tin, and a sooty fireplace and a woodbox along one wall, a table, enough chairs, and long windows you could look out and see down the road. We sat around the oil-clothed table holding our feet off the damp floor. The clean boards smelled of lye. The stove was cold. Bird had put away all the pans except her round one; it sat on the warmer, piled with rice and peas. While she stepped around the wet spots in bare feet and wrung out the mop, we told about the fun we'd had—how we'd climbed all over that machine. Even Maggie had gone up halfway.

"Fiddle and bow time," Bird said and smiled. "Better enjoy it now, 'cause a little bit more and school'll be starting. Then it's the shovel and hoe." She squinted at Maggie. "For you too, Miss Lady."

Maggie giggled. She would be going to school for the first time in September and talked about it all the time, even though she was scared. She still half-believed Bird's story about a tiny fiddle and bow resting in a cubby-hole spot above one kitchen window, and a shovel and hoe above another. Maggie loved to hear her tell how one set would slowly come out when the other was disappearing; these things only Bird could see. "Is it happening, Bird? Can you see the shovel and hoe yet?" she asked, deliciously afraid.

Bird tilted back her head and peered at the cubby-hole. "No, I don't see nothing yet." Then she stared out a window, and her voice changed to a low sound. "I don't see Mizell coming up the road neither. He's supposed to pick up my pay."

My stomach felt funny. I remembered how I'd laughed that Sunday, and now Bird had to wait to get her money.

Gil walked to the window and stood by her, gazing out. "Maybe he's gone to town, Bird, to get some stuff for his trip." He turned toward her. "If he doesn't come, or Gus, Papa'll give you your money. I know he will." Gus was Bird's husband and he worked in a turpentine camp. He might be gone a week or two, then one evening we'd see him coming up the road, swinging an old railroad lantern. He'd walk Bird home. But he hadn't been around for a while.

"Yes, I reckon," Bird said, leaving the window, her eyes down. She pulled her high-top tennis shoes from under the table and sat in a straight chair by Maggie to put them on. When she leaned over to tie the laces, her goiter swayed under the sleeve of her dress. It jiggled as if it were alive. Maggie reached and lightly touched the spot. "That feels so soft, Bird. Does it hurt?"

"Don't know it's there." Smiling, she straightened.

❧

It was late Sunday afternoon. We were playing in the woods near the road-scraper, mainly to stay out of the house. Bird hadn't shown up that morning, hadn't even sent word, and Mother was in a snit. After church Papa had taken us to the S & W Cafeteria—it was new in town and the only place open on Sunday, but Mother hadn't liked it, said the okra and tomatoes were tasteless. When we got home she motioned to Papa, "Frank, I want to speak with you alone." Mother led him down the hall toward the back porch. "You know she's drinking, of course," we heard her say.

We had trailed out to the front yard, passed the shady part, and gone on to the sunny clearing. If Gil was worried about what Mother was saying to Papa, he didn't let on. We climbed on the road-scraper, but the sun was so hot the metal burned. Then we moved to the woods just behind and made a lean-to out of pine branches; Gil bossed Maggie and me, telling us to get bigger limbs. I didn't care. It took my mind off Bird. We were still piling on branches when Papa walked from the house and headed toward our maroon Chevy, parked in the wide dirt space under the big oaks.

"Where're you going?" hollered Gil. "Can we come?"

I stopped, waiting for the answer, a bunch of green pine needles in my hand.

"Bird's," said Papa, his hand on the car door. He motioned to us. Maybe he was going give Bird a good talking to, I thought, running to the car.

Usually when we rode with him to Bird's house on some errand—taking her wire for a chicken coop or something—we'd go in with him. Bird didn't mind us traipsing through her rooms, looking at the old calendars and pictures of Jesus on the wall, those we could see in the dim light. But what we liked best was her yard; she kept frizzy chickens, a guinea, and a dog or two. This evening, though, when we stopped on the side of the road, Papa told us to stay in the car. I sat on the edge of the back seat by Gil and watched Papa step across the shallow ditch, open the wire gate, and walk up on the porch. The door was closed. Daylight was getting thin, and the inside of the house looked dark. "Bur-rid," Papa called, the way he usually did. He knocked, but the door stayed closed. He knocked a long time, and then it opened just a slit. Papa talked at the slit. When the opening became wider, he stepped in. They didn't close the door, but it was so shadowy inside we could see only the outline of things. My heart beat fast. Papa was lecturing Bird to please Mother, I told myself, and in a minute it would be over. At first I kept quiet because Gil doesn't like to talk about troubles, even small ones. But after a minute or two, I touched his arm. "Do you think Papa's going to fuss at Bird much?" I asked. "I hope it's just a little, and nobody gets fired."

Maggie was in the front, and she put in her two bits. "You know what Mother said. One more time."

"Shut up, Maggie," Gil said. "What do you know? You ain't even been to school yet."

"I do know something." She twisted in the seat and gave him a big-eyed stare.

"No, you don't. Big-mouth! That's what you are."

"I'm not a big-mouth!"

"He's probably seeing if Bird's sick."

"But he didn't take her anything."

"Know-it-all. Blabber mouth!"

Maggie tuned up. "I'm not a blabber mouth. I don't want him to fire Bird either," she wailed.

We sat awhile longer. Maggie stopped sniffing. Then Gil decided it was all right to get out of the car as long as we stayed in the road and didn't go near the house. In a few minutes we moved just inside Bird's yard, but stayed away from the porch. The chickens weren't in sight, but one of the dogs lay on the ground, and lightning bugs were beginning to come out. They flashed their yellow fire on and off, bright as little flashlights. Laughing, we chased them.

"These are easy to catch!" Gil grabbed one and held it in his cupped hand.

"They's always low and easy at first dark," someone called from the porch. "Later on, when it gets night, they'll be higher and higher. Ain't no catching them then." It was Bird, leaning in the doorway. Her voice sounded funny, sleepy and gruff, and I'd never seen her look so tired—eyelids drooping, hair matted, no cap on. Even her goiter seemed to sag, as if it were tired too.

We froze, lightning bugs in our hands. We stood there forever. Then Gil said, "Hello, Bird," calm as could be.

"Hey, Gil, Baby." Bird took a swaying step forward. Papa appeared from behind, put his hand on her shoulder, and guided her back in. Through the half-opened door we saw him sit her down and place a lighted lamp on a table beside her.

When he came out, Papa told us to get in the car, and we drove a short piece down the road to Irving Jones's house. Irving was Bird's cousin. Before Papa went in, he told us not to budge out of the car this time and he meant it.

We sat, Maggie staring out the windshield, and Gil and I in the back. Finally, I poked Gil and asked, "Do you think he fired her?"

"No. Nothing's wrong." Gil pushed back his dark hair like he was angry at me for asking and shook his head.

But on the way home, Gil surprised me. He leaned forward, propping his arms on the back of Papa's seat, and asked, "Is Bird all right? Is she coming to work tomorrow?"

Papa kept his eyes on the road, on the slanting yellow path made by the headlight. "Bird's not feeling good, but she'll be all right. Mizell's gone, but Gus'll be home in a day or two, and Irving is going to look in on her. I told her to take some time off."

"Take some time off?" Gil pulled back his head and sat straight. "How long?"

Papa didn't say.

"Who's gonna cook for us now, Papa?" piped Maggie, sitting sideways, one hand on the dashboard. "Who'll we get?"

"Oh, hush up," snapped Gil. He stretched one leg over and pushed against the back of her seat, making her tilt forward.

"Bird won't be out long," I said over Maggie's squeal. I hoped that was true. Mother really liked Bird, when she wasn't drinking. "She'll be back soon."

We rolled into the yard. The lightning bugs were high now, out of reach, twinkling on and off in the lower tree branches like tiny Christmas lights. On the far side of the clearing sat the road-scraper, a huge, tangled-up shadow—long octopus arms at crazy angles, wheels twisted, the top umbrella turned into a scarecrow's black hat.

Gilbert jumped out, slamming the door. He ran toward the machine, then stopped and wheeled around toward Maggie, who was putting her feet on the ground. He spread his arms and made a face like a monster. "That thing's gonna get you, Maggie," he shouted. "It's gonna get you because you're a *big-mouth!*"

"Make him stop," Maggie called to Papa.

"Now, Son," Papa said, coming around the front of the car. His hand was out as though he was about to reach for Gil.

But Gil was already running toward the steps. He yelled over his shoulder, "I was just telling her what she needs to know."

"That blade can cut the ground out from under you," I said, talking low. I started for the house, then walked back and took Maggie's small damp hand. "Like Bird said," I breathed to her. "Just like Bird."

The Sky Blue Studebaker ᴖ

When Gilbert was young, his face was open and innocent. His smile stretched his mouth into a wide curve that showed small, spaced teeth. It seemed to say he was in charge of his world, and for a while he was. Our world—his and Maggie's and mine—was cut off from town by four long miles, and that suited Gil fine. He loved to ramble, and rambling was no problem. He would walk or ride his bike.

Then he turned thirteen and learned to drive. I was ten, the oldest girl, still playing with Maggie in the doll house. Maggie was seven. One Sunday in January on the way home from church, Papa turned off the highway and stopped our old maroon Chevy on the side of the hard-packed dirt road. He swapped places with Gil. Maggie and I were in the back with Mother and we hollered, "Drive, Gil!" Wearing a wide-brimmed lavender hat, Mother tilted her head to tell Papa she thought Gil was too young, but she didn't say it hard like she meant it, so Papa let him drive. After that, Gil was under the wheel every chance he got. Mostly he circled the yard, but sometimes he drove down the road as far as Bird's house.

A year or so before, Bird, our cook, was fired for eight long months. Then Papa said her drinking was better. We all clapped—even Mother smiled—when Bird walked back into our kitchen, like the Prodigal

Son returning. On Saturdays, if Bird ran late finishing the dishes, Papa let Gil drive her home.

One Saturday in March, after our Chevy had broken down for the third time, Papa announced at the dinner table that we would soon buy a new car. Gilbert gave his happy Jack-o'-lantern smile. Later, in the kitchen, he bragged to Bird while she washed the dishes that before long he'd be driving her home in a new car—a shiny Ford, maybe. I was helping Bird's granddaughter clear the table; her name was Earlene, but Bird called her Dollbaby and so did we. When I pushed through the swinging door with the rice bowl, I heard Gil whisper to Bird, as if they were in a conspiracy, "Today, though, I can drive you home in the old one if you're running late. So wash slow."

Gil had all the fun, I thought. "Here's the rice bowl, the last one, and I'm not handing it to you slow." I screwed up my face and set it on the kitchen table with a clunk.

"Go on. Get some more, Elizabeth," said Gil, sticking out his neck and smiling.

Bird let out a low chuckle and dipped her brown fingers into the enamel dishpan nestled in the long white sink. Dollbaby strolled in with two plates and Bird said, "Crumb the dining table now, Dollbaby, and bring me the fruit bowl on the sideboard so I can wash it too."

After she finished, I watched them roll out of the yard—Bird and Dollbaby in back, and Gil sitting straight and gripping the wheel of the old Chevrolet as though he were ready to drive right on to the city limits if they wanted to go that far.

Later, car salesmen drove out from town in new Chevrolets, Fords, Plymouths. When giving directions, Papa would tell them where to turn off the highway and say they couldn't miss our house—the dirt road ended under the trees in our front yard. I always felt that the road began there, but I guess saying it like that would have mixed them up.

If we were home from school when one of the sleek new automobiles rounded the curve, we would stop playing and watch it pull up under the oaks in our front yard, tires crunching the acorns. We would circle the car admiring the color or the curve of the bumper, while Papa, wearing a long-sleeved shirt and his tie tucked in under the second button, talked to the salesman. Papa was in no hurry to decide. Maggie wanted him to get the Ford because the salesman winked at her and gave her gum. Mother thought we should stick with a dependable Chevrolet. I didn't care much, and just listened to Gil lecture on the advantages of each model. Usually he liked the last one he'd seen.

"How do you know which one is best, smartie?" asked Maggie, hands on hips, her sandy-brown bangs touching the wrinkles in her forehead. We were standing on the front porch watching a shiny black Plymouth pull out of the yard.

Gil smirked, including me in his satisfied look even though I hadn't said anything. "At least I can drive."

Before Easter we had a week's vacation from school. The first day, after breakfast, Gil and I ran to the far side of the front yard beyond the dirt oval where cars parked and began taking turns on the wire slide—a wonderful thing Papa had set up. He'd threaded a heavy wire through a short piece of metal pipe, then stretched the wire between two strong oaks, starting fairly high in one and slanting to near the roots of the other. At the second oak Papa had wrapped the wire around a nail and hammered it into the bark. One of us children would climb the boards nailed to the first tree, then grab the pipe, hang on with legs dangling, and scoot down the wire. It was fun. We had to be careful to plant our feet on the ground at exactly the right moment or we might smash into the rough tree trunk at the bottom. The pipe had a string attached, and after each ride down, the one finishing could sling it up the wire to the next rider, waiting at the top.

"Here, Gil," I called. I had just flown down the wire and was ready to shoot the pipe up to him in the tree.

"Elizabeth, look!" He pointed over my head. A car was gliding up the dirt road toward us, chrome gleaming in the sunlight. We watched it roll into the oak-shaded clearing between us and the house.

"How you like that one?" I sang out.

"Man, I hope Papa gets it. That's a Studebaker."

The car, sky blue and graceful as a cloud, came to a stop under the trees. The hood ornament was a windswept **S**, silver, like the curved bumper. The **S** made it seem monogrammed for us—Spencer, our last name. Just sitting there the car made me think of a bird ready to fly. "It looks so light," I said.

Gil zipped down the slide, holding his feet bunched under him instead of dangling, and we raced to the car.

While Papa talked to the salesman, Gil checked out the tires and the radiator grill. Opening the door, I breathed in the cool, new-car smell. Everything was pale blue-gray, from the leather-trimmed seats to the felt lining at the top. I ran my hand along the padding of the door—smooth, like the inside of an oyster shell. "It's so pretty!" I said.

"I bet it runs good too." Gil slid into the driver's seat and touched the gear shift, a new kind that was attached to the shaft of the steering wheel. "Hey, I like this," he said, wiggling the gear.

I sat in the passenger seat beside him. Wrinkling my nose, I patted the blue-gray upholstery. "Doesn't it smell wonderful? Better than the Chevrolet."

"Smells better than strawberry shortcake," said Gil, laughing. That was his favorite. He jumped out and ran to Papa, who was sitting on the thick mossy root with the salesman, both with papers balanced on their knees. Gil asked him to buy the car right away.

Papa shook his head and handed the papers back. He wrote down some figures, though.

Two days later, when he made the deal, Gil and I were a mile away. We'd gone frog gigging at the pond near Pallbearers' Cemetery. Gil often rode his bike there, hanging a bucket on the handlebars and carrying his gig—a wooden shaft with four metal prongs at the end. Usually I didn't go with him, but nothing else was going on that morning so he let me climb onto the back of his bike. Balancing the gig on my shoulder, I held to his waist as we rode over the rib-like bumps. Near the cemetery the road turned into packed-down red clay, and on that part the bicycle tires purred.

Gil couldn't find any frogs. I was glad because the last time I'd gone with him, he handed me a bullfrog that was still kicking and told me to hit it against a tree trunk until it stopped wiggling. Mostly I lay on the bank while he thrashed through the squashy edge of the pond, jabbing at anything that moved. The air was hot and sort of smelly; a dead fish was rotting somewhere. Pretty soon Gil got tired. Night was the best time for gigging—he knew that—when you could blind the frog with a flashlight.

On the way home, I held to Gil's waist and angled the gig out in front, pointed end up, like a devil might carry his pitchfork. I was jiggling it as we wheeled around the curve, and our shady front yard came into view.

"Look!" yelled Gil, slowing down. I peeked around his back. Ahead, the blue car sat calmly under the oaks as if posed for a magazine ad. "It's *ours*," said Gil.

First thing, he talked Papa into taking us for a ride. Then he talked Papa into telling him how everything worked, and, finally, into letting him drive. Gil circled the yard a dozen times and by suppertime he could handle the Studebaker, could change gears smooth. But when it came time to take Bird home, Papa sat in the front seat beside him.

The next day Gil chauffeured Bird home alone. "He drives good as you, Mr. Frank," she said the next morning at breakfast, setting the white grits bowl on Papa's right. Maggie and I giggled, and Papa looked like he might grin. "Backed up and turned around like he been doing it all his life," Bird bragged.

On Saturday, the day before Easter, Papa said Gil could take the car to go frog gigging if he would first trim the dead branches off both grape arbors. While Gil cut vines in the big arbor, Maggie and I settled in the kitchen. Bird walked in and out, and Dollbaby, in a red dress, sat by the window shelling black-eyed peas. The chair had a split in the seat so her bottom sagged through in a bright round bulge. Dollbaby was a year younger than I, and had full, dimpled cheeks and plump arms, her skin a shade darker than Bird's. She couldn't talk real plain. We liked to get her started telling something and then tease her. Soon we squatted beside her and began shelling peas into the blue bowl too, listening to her describe the Easter play to be given at her church on Sunday. She had a part—one line to say.

"Say it for us," begged Maggie, running her finger inside a pod.

Dollbaby dropped the peas, clasped her stubby hands, and said in a loud sing-song, "Je-sus rose on Eat-ta Day."

We laughed, rocking back on our heels. Maggie tilted her head, just like Mother, and said, "It's *Easter* day, Dollbaby. Say it again."

"Jesus rose on Eat-ta day!" proclaimed Dollbaby. We kept asking her to say it over and over and laughing until Bird walked in from the back porch. She made us stop. Then Maggie and I ran outside to take turns on the wire slide.

Sunlight danced through the openings in the tree branches, and we zoomed down the wire, feeling like spot-lighted circus performers under a green canopy. After a few times, though, we noticed the wire was getting slack. Just as I finished a ride, the bottom end came loose. We did our best to fix it back, but the nail had come out, so we had to knot the wire around the tree trunk. Neither of us wanted to take the first test run. We were sitting on the ground debating when Dollbaby came around the side of the house, walking like she had all day and tomorrow. She crossed the front yard, grinning, and dusted her hands to show us she was finished shelling peas and was ready to play.

"Dollbaby," Maggie said, syrupy sweet, "if you say your piece for us again, we'll let you take the next ride. We're just resting."

"Jesus rose on Eat-ta day!" she shouted over her shoulder, loping toward the tree with the board steps.

Luckily the knot didn't give until she was half-way down. Still, the fall knocked the wind out of her and scared Maggie and me plenty. We knelt over her as she lay stretched out on the hard ground, unable to catch her breath, her red skirt up to her waist. Maggie started blubbering about how she hoped Dollbaby wasn't hurt bad and how we shouldn't have tried to fix the wire ourselves. I said I was sorry and begged her not to tell. But Dollbaby told Bird, and Bird told Mother.

"I hope you'll remember this and learn a lesson," said Mother, one hand posted on her hip. I think she could see how scared we were. She turned to Maggie. "And remember too, Miss Lady, it wasn't so long ago that you said 'Hello-bean' for Halloween." She pointed toward the kitchen. "You both go and apologize to Earlene and then sweep the porches."

We made a full repentance. Sitting in the sagging kitchen chair, Dollbaby rubbed her back, but she could hardly keep a straight face. "You sure you sorry?" she asked.

Dinner was at noon, and afterward, while Maggie and I were finishing the front steps, Gil paraded out with his gig and bucket in

one hand, car keys in the other. In the doorway behind him stood
Mother, arms crossed, mouth twisted to show she wasn't pleased.

"One side, Eliz-a-beth," Gil said. I was sweeping the middle step,
Maggie the bottom one. He jingled the two car keys, held together by
a string. "You too, Maggie."

Right then I could have kicked him in the seat. We watched him
start up the blue Studebaker, saw it lurch once and take off.

Later—a lot later, it seemed—he rolled into the yard. The sun was
getting low. From the front bedroom window I saw him pull up close
to the oak with the big, buckling roots. The car looked so pretty, gliding to a stop, but Gil piled out in such a hurry, my attention went to
him, not the car. He skirted the side of the house, taking the path by
the wisteria-covered fence, and headed toward the back. The way he
walked—kind of secretive, head down and gripping the gig hard
enough to break it—made me know something was wrong. I started to
call but he rounded the corner where the house does a turn and spreads
out. That's where the kitchen wing was once added on, Bird had told
us. Gil was going to the kitchen steps, I figured. I slipped out the front
door and walked quietly to the dirt oval where the car was parked.

The last of the afternoon sun sifted through the oak branches and
the Studebaker rested in a pool of light. It looked as grand as ever.
Slowly, I circled the front to see if there were any scratches. It's just a
car, I told myself, and stepped toward the back end, thinking I'd find a
dent. But the sky blue body was as smooth as a still lake. I could see
my oblong reflection in the door—a stretched-out face with straggly,
mud-colored hair. I pushed back a stray piece, wishing for auburn hair,
or blonde, or even rich dark brown hair, like Gil's.

But I didn't think about hair long. The front window was open and
I leaned in. I let out a gasp. Behind the driver's seat a loose piece of
blue-gray cloth hung down. I looked up at an ugly three-cornered tear
in the top lining; the material dangled like a flap of skin from a butch-
ered animal.

I felt sick. "Oh, Gilbert," I said aloud and ran my fingers along the
jagged edges.

Bird heard it first. I wasn't in the kitchen when Gil told what hap-

pened—how he'd stayed a little longer than he meant to, and when
he threw his stuff in the car, how he shoved the gig in too quick and it
tore the top all at once, and then there was nothing he could do but
drive home, tell, and take the punishment. Bird said he started to cry
and she almost couldn't get him to stop. I'm glad I wasn't there. Later,
it was bad enough hearing Mother's and Papa's voices rumbling in the
next room and Gil's asking more than once, "Can't it be fixed?" His
high, tense voice came through the bedroom wall and reached me
where I sat in a straight-backed chair. Finally I put my fingers in my
ears. If only I could wish that tear away.

On Easter morning Papa drove us to church. The inside of the car still
smelled leathery and new, but in the top lining a large safety pin held
the cloth flap in place. It looked like a homemade stitch on a raw
wound. No one mentioned it. The night before, Papa had insisted on
a truce and even gave Gil an encouraging talk. Riding in, though,
Mother sat in the back between Maggie and me where she could see
the tear good. Her lips were pressed together, and I knew she was
holding back an "I told you so."

Before we turned onto the highway, we passed the white wooden
church where Bird and Dollbaby went on Sundays. The bell in its
squat steeple clanged; service was starting. Maggie looked out the window and let out a low giggle. "Jesus rose on Eat-ta Day!" she said, just
like Dollbaby.

I couldn't laugh. I kept watching Gil's reflection in the front window, his head turned toward the glass. His dark hair lay limply on his
forehead and his face looked empty, as though something had been
swept away. All the way to church I tried to think of some words to say
to him but I couldn't.

On Monday, Papa took the car to a garage in town. The man, he
later told us, tried hard, pulled at the cloth trying to fit the torn edges
together. Then he said to just leave the safety pin in; it worked as well
as anything. When Papa told us, I almost cried. We were stuck with
that shiny pin. Gil was stuck most of all. It was hard for me to believe
that something caused by such a quick little accident couldn't be fixed.

After a few days of moping, Gil livened up. He smiled again, but instead of his happy Jack-o'-lantern smile, he picked up the habit of smiling with his lips closed, hiking one side of his mouth.

We kept the Studebaker a long time. The sky blue color hardly faded. The **S** hood ornament stayed in place. I learned to drive in it, Maggie too, and Gil drove it on dates until he left for the Navy. Although we took the car to several more garages, they all said the same thing—no patch job could really fix that three-cornered tear. The silver safety pin stayed. It held the rough-edged pieces of blue cloth almost together, but not quite.

Four Miles ᕽ

"You can't just *walk* to town," Elizabeth said to Isabel, one of her birthday party guests. "It's too far!"

They were standing by the back yard fence, away from the other girls, Elizabeth in her Saturday clothes—corduroy pants and a pink sweater. This wasn't a dress-up party. They were all eleven, or close to it, and I was still seven—not old enough to be one of them, but hanging around, pretending not to listen. I kicked at a plank in the fence. The fence used to be white; now it was no-color. I accidentally loosened a board.

"I can make it," announced Isabel, one hand on her hip.

"But if you leave the party," pleaded Elizabeth, "you'll get in trouble."

"I don't care. I'm not going to stay anywhere with *her* around." Isabel jerked her head toward the back steps, where four girls sat, talking and petting Gil's old spotted setter. I knew which one was "her"— Caroline, the pretty, dark-haired girl in the full red skirt. Besides Isabel, who had on something pleated and flowered, she was the only one who'd worn a skirt. About a dozen other sixth-graders, in pants, jumped rope near the playhouse.

"Caroline didn't mean to hurt your feelings. Anyway, town is four miles!" Elizabeth made four miles sound as far as the moon.

"She *did* mean it. She's a snot." Isabel threw her head back and her curly blond hair jiggled. "I'll catch a ride, hitchhike."

I snickered.

Elizabeth whipped around, her brown eyes narrowing. "Maggie, get away!"

"I'm not paying any attention," I said. Bending, I shoved the board back onto its rusty nail. I moved a step away and began to pick up acorns, choosing them carefully, as though looking for a special one. I wanted to see what would happen. I'd heard Caroline brag that a boy named Leonard was coming to see her a lot, that Isabel had lost out because she was too fat. She didn't say it to Isabel, but someone must have told her. That's why she called Caroline a snot.

"Please stay." Elizabeth grabbed Isabel's arm. "Mrs. Watts'll be here soon to pick you up."

"I'm not getting in a car with that liar either. I might hit her." Isabel wrinkled her face. She looked like a riled-up bumble-bee.

"You can go back in the other car then."

"Listen. If I stay here any longer there's liable to be an explosion." Isabel swung her arms like she was warming up for a fight.

An explosion! I kicked acorns and pictured a corn-cob fight in the barn. We'd had one the Sunday before when Gil's friends and mine came for the afternoon. But the boys started it and my friends and I mostly hopped around and dodged. It was fun. I wasn't sure what happened when girls exploded. Did they wrestle and roll in the dirt?

"I'm leaving. If anything happens to me, she'll be sorry." Isabel prissed to the saggy wooden gate. "I hope something *does* happen," she threw back.

"Wait!" Elizabeth ran to her, then craned around Isabel's back at me. "Maggie, I told you to get away."

"You don't own this yard," I grumbled, straggling toward the porch. Before I was out of earshot, I heard Elizabeth whisper again, "Isabel, you can't walk to town by yourself."

❧

Instead of just walking out the gate, they must have gone over the stile that our cook, Bird, climbed over when she came into our yard. It was near the pump house, almost hidden. I didn't actually see them leave.

I'd stopped at the back steps to show those girls how Pat, Gil's setter, could grin. If you petted the very top of his head and tickled him under the chin, he'd stretch his mouth into a silly smile. The girls hooted. Caroline arranged her red skirt and bent to try it. When I glanced toward the fence—no Elizabeth or Isabel. Beyond the pecan grove, in the curving dirt road, I could see two figures clipping along, close to the ditch. Isabel's flowered skirt bounced. Elizabeth in her neat dark pants looked tiny beside her, but she kept in step. Isabel *was* a little fat, I decided.

I started to say, "Hey, look at them!" to the girls on the steps. I thought of finding Mother. But as I watched, arms folded, Elizabeth and Isabel made the curve and disappeared behind the trees. I found myself grinning like Pat. Elizabeth didn't do stuff like this! Besides leaving her party guests, she would really upset Mother. I couldn't imagine her and Isabel walking all the way to town though. Bird walked it sometimes, and Dollbaby, her granddaughter, did every Saturday, but they were used to it. Elizabeth and Isabel would turn around at the crossroads and come back, I figured. Then I'd get to see the explosion. Black eyes, ripped clothes!

Mary Louise, Elizabeth's best friend, skipped on skinny legs to the steps where I sat perched beside the four girls. She smiled and her mouth looked like a jungle gym. Mary Louise had worn braces forever. "Where's Elizabeth?" she asked, lisping a little.

I was about to say, "She's left! With Isabel, and they're going to *walk* to town." Mary Louise's eyes were going to pop out. But before I could open my mouth, Caroline pushed back her long black hair and said, "Look, Mary Lou, see how I can make this dog grin." She petted and tickled until old Pat stretched his mouth, and Mary Louise laughed. I was glad I hadn't told. I felt smarter than anyone. They didn't have any idea what was going on.

I leaned back on the steps and pictured Elizabeth and Isabel walking down the middle of the sunny dirt road, getting to the crossroads, and then to the Morgans' house that sat on the left up under some wide trees with thick mossy roots. The last time I'd been at the Morgans was on Halloween. Gil, Elizabeth, and I had on old pillowcases with eye holes cut out; we acted like ghosts, whooing, waving our arms, and making huge shadows on the wall. The Morgan children's excited faces shone in the firelight. They knew who it was, but they still hollered and hid behind Hattie Morgan's skirts.

Elizabeth and Isabel weren't going to turn around at the crossroads, it now seemed. Were they really going to walk to town? Wouldn't they get tired? Could two little white girls make it that far? Sure, I thought. Elizabeth was as strong as Dollbaby, any day. Smart too.

"Where's Isabel?" asked freckled Pauline, getting up from the steps. She was the tallest sixth-grader. Pauline stretched to her full height, and I looked at Caroline, the pretty snot, to see if she'd say something mean about Isabel. She lifted the corner of her mouth but she kept on talking to Mary Louise and stroking Pat. Well, Pauline, I thought, *I* could answer that.

I tickled old Pat myself. Elizabeth and Isabel would be past the low spot in the road now, where the dirt turned sandy and the Bridge Pond during heavy rains flowed up to the ruts. They were getting to the Acre, the place where Bird lived. On the Acre was a tiny store, a church where they sang better than in our church, and five or six houses, their yards swept and geraniums in cans on the front steps. I knew everybody on the Acre. I even knew their dogs.

On the way to school each morning, Gil, Elizabeth, and I had a contest to see who could count the most dogs. With Papa driving, Gil would sit up front, and he and Elizabeth would take one side of the road; I'd take the other. The left side was the best because the house next to Bird's, Tug Bailey's, had four old dogs that slept on the porch. Elizabeth and I had to watch Gil to be sure he didn't count a dog under a house that he really couldn't see. He was bad about that. Claimed he could see a tail.

By this time—about four o'clock I figured—most folks on the Acre had already walked to town. They wouldn't see Isabel and Elizabeth hiking down the road where the whitish dirt turned brown—past the store, past the church—but I wished they could. Elizabeth might even meet Dollbaby on the way back home. Dollbaby liked to make a big fuss. She'd holler, pretend to faint. I laughed to myself.

"Time for Pin-The-Tail-On-The-Donkey!" Mother sang out. "Then the cake." She was on the screened-in part of the back porch, spreading a white cloth over a table that would hold the punch. On the wall hung a drawing of a no-tail donkey that was cutting his eyes in her direction, as if he knew a secret.

I moved to the top step so I'd be first. Mother folded a white handkerchief into a blindfold. As she bent to arrange the donkey tails and pins on a straight chair, I could see the nape of her neck, where her brown braids crossed. Some mornings I watched her fix her hair—plait it, wrap the braids around her head, then pin them tight, like she meant business. I had a sinking feeling. She would ask *me* where Elizabeth was. If I lied I'd be caught. She'd give me a glare that could freeze boiling water; then I'd have to sit in a chair for no telling how long. If I tattled, she'd be mad because I hadn't told sooner. Shrinking, I slid down to the bottom step. Then I inched over and sat on the ground under the edge of the porch, the way I did when it rained. Mother wouldn't look here. In the yard the girls were playing "May I." One of them called to "It" by the oak tree, "May I take three giant steps?" "It" leaned her back against the trunk and said, "You may." I smirked, thinking what if Elizabeth and Isabel had asked if they could please walk to town? "It" would have said no, you forgot to say "May I." They surely hadn't said, "May I," not to Mother or anybody.

Now, they'd be close to the highway, the hardroad. Before you got to the pavement, on one side was St. Philip's Chapel—white, with a squatty steeple. It was where Bird and Dollbaby walked to on the first and third Sundays and where Dollbaby said her pieces. On the opposite side was Sylvester Williams's little patched-up house. He owned a brown dog and a rooster Gil claimed he could hear before daybreak in the summer. Elizabeth believed him, but I didn't think he could because Sylvester's house was a mile away.

In my mind I saw Elizabeth and Isabel pass Sylvester's (a lazy dog curled up by the steps) and swing onto the hardroad. They'd walk on the left shoulder, facing the cars riding toward Ousley. But if Isabel wanted to hitchhike, they'd have to cross to the other side. I hoped Isabel wouldn't stick out her thumb. Gil did that once, the only time he ran away. The truck that stopped was heading for Texas, the driver said, and Texas sounded so big and far he didn't climb into the cab.

"Eliz-a-beth," shouted Mother. She was at the top of the steps, and I could see her low-heeled black pumps side-by-side. "Elizabeth!"

"Isabel's not here either," said Mary Louise on the bottom step.

"Maybe they're at the barn," Pauline said, and she ran to see. Above me, feet scraped, but the voices didn't sound worried. Feeling pretty safe, I peeked out. Mother paced down the porch, past the no-tail donkey that seemed to follow her with his eyes. At the punch bowl she turned around and I dropped back to my knees. I could imagine her expression when she found out—mouth straight, wrinkled forehead, like, well, I can't believe God has given me such bad children! I could already hear her lecturing Elizabeth: "Leaving your *own* birthday party!"

Feet ran on the porch. Girls twittered. Nobody could find Elizabeth. Isabel either!

"Maggie!" Mother shouted. Then, not waiting for me to answer, I heard her order one of the girls to look for Papa. I sat still, beginning to feel scared for Elizabeth, scared even for me. Folks said I was Mother's favorite. Maybe I was. When we sat with Mother in the hall rocker, I'd be in her lap and Elizabeth would ride her foot, not minding that I had the best spot. When you ride the foot, I thought, walking four miles to town was extra risky. Still, Elizabeth had dared to walk.

Now, they'd be stepping through the low weeds on the road's shoulder, getting sandspurs. I imagined Isabel picking them from her socks and fussing. Soon they'd pass the McConnells' house with its sagging, plant-filled porch. The McConnells were Bird's cousins. No dogs, just one black-and-white cat. But we never counted cats.

"Maggie, where are you?" Mother tramped down the steps, arms swinging. She looked the other way from where I squatted. In front of me was the place where, during rains, water funneled down and made a dip in the ground—good for wading. She turned and I wished it was another day and I was up to my ankles in water. I crawled out. Mother fixed me with an anxious stare. "Mother," I began, dusting off my pants. But before I could think of what to say next, Caroline touched Mother's elbow with a finger and said in a whispery voice, "Mrs. Spencer, I saw two girls walking down the road a while ago—there." She pointed toward the curve, acting like she didn't know who they were. "It must have been them. I thought they'd be right back, but you know how Isabel is." She gave a tiny shrug. "She didn't want to stay. They may be walking to town."

Well, the snot had saved my hide. But I couldn't believe she'd seen them too, then sat smugly making old Pat grin. She must have wanted Isabel in trouble. Probably not Elizabeth, but then she didn't know my mother when she got mad—how it would be at the supper table, Mother sitting straight in her chair, lips tight, and none of us, not even Papa, saying anything except "Please pass the butter." Elizabeth might throw up. She'd done that once.

I hung by the rain dip while Mother hurried across the porch, apologizing to the girls, calling for Frank, my Papa. The girls ran around, more excited than they'd been all day.

"Mother," I said, finally tipping up the steps. "Elizabeth isn't so bad. I think Isabel made her do it."

Mother whipped around. "Do you think they're actually walking to town? Or hiding?"

"Maybe walking. But don't be mad. I hope they don't get into a truck going to Texas."

"Goodness!" Mother touched her chest, then motioned to Mary Louise. "Please serve the cake, dear. Pour punch! Mr. Spencer must be in the cantaloupe patch." She dashed into the hall. In a minute, our blue Studebaker shot out of the front yard and found the ruts in the road. I watched it make the curve and disappear. By now Elizabeth and Isabel should be as far as the slanting green house with the tiny porch where a worn-looking white woman washed clothes in the back yard. One scrawny black dog. Part of me wished they'd made it all the way.

"We got almost to the City Limits," Isabel bragged to a skinny sixth-grader who was still eating cake. They angled toward Mrs. Roberts's black Packard, which had driven up in the front yard a few minutes after Mother. Mrs. Watts had been right behind. The women had the car doors open, loading girls for the trip back. Two more girls ran up to Isabel, asking questions. Caroline sat primly in the front of Mrs. Watts's green sedan, staring out the window. Elizabeth was in the hall, where Mother had sent her.

"Good-bye, girls," Mother waved from the porch, stretching her lips over her teeth in what was supposed to be a smile. I stood at her elbow. I could feel her twitch. Isabel, her flowered skirt swinging as she walked, had the nerve to turn and call, "I had a nice time, Mrs. Spencer." Mother shot her such a look I was surprised Isabel didn't wilt to the ground.

Then Mrs. Watts motioned, and Mother walked out to her car. Quickly I ran into the house.

Elizabeth sat in a straight chair by the hall tree, her eyes downcast. But she was just barely swinging a foot, as though she still hadn't quite stopped walking.

"Did you really get to the City Limits?" I asked solemnly, as I might talk to someone on Death Row.

Elizabeth gave me a sideways look. "No, we only got to that red house with those two spotted puppies. You know."

I nodded. "Did you meet Dollbaby?"

"No, but I wondered if we would." She almost smiled. "Isabel jumped the ditch when Mother pulled up."

"She did?"

"Tried to get me to jump too. Then she ran into a field and I had to chase her."

"Elizabeth!"

"Mother got pretty mad. Wouldn't talk, driving us back."

"She'll calm down," I whispered. "All you'll get is some sitting down time."

"I'm going to get a spanking," said Elizabeth.

I couldn't think of a thing to say. I'd never gotten a spanking.

I was sitting cross-legged in the back porch swing when I heard it— the whap, whap, whap of the rick-rack paddle. Mother and Elizabeth were on the sleeping porch, close behind me. "Leaving your *own*

party!" I heard Mother say. Three more whaps. This was only the second spanking that I knew of at our house—first, Gil when he ran away. Mother spanked him hard. He hollered some, but not Elizabeth. I think Elizabeth must have made up her mind, back there at the fence even before they set out, that she'd just have to take her medicine. I doubted that Isabel had done that, and she was getting off. No fair!

Behind me the door opened. Elizabeth walked out on the porch ahead of Mother, a procession of two. A few tears streaked her face, but she calmly sat down beside me in the swing. Elizabeth was brave!

Mother marched to the far end of the porch and lifted the cake plate off the table. Behind her on the wall was the donkey with one tail pinned right on the tip of his nose. On the plate lay a hunk of white cake; a knife, messy with icing, stuck out the side as though it had been stabbed.

Mother stepped over some wrapped presents on the floor. Then she looked toward the swing.

Now Elizabeth will get the rest of her sentence, I thought—how long she'd have to stay inside and sit in a chair. All day, and tomorrow. Into next week. Why couldn't Mother let one punishment be enough?

Mother stared at the swing, her mouth still in a line, but it didn't seem quite so set. "Do you want a piece of your cake, Elizabeth? Not that you deserve it."

"Yes ma'am." Her answer was soft.

"Me, too," I said, not looking at Mother too straight, sneaking a quick glance, like the donkey.

In a minute we sat shoulder-to-shoulder in the swing eating cake, Mother in the middle. "Imagine, two *ten*-year-olds getting into a fuss over a boy. And running away!" said Mother, pushing her foot hard against the straw mat to make the swing go.

"Eleven," I ventured. "This is Elizabeth's birthday."

"Eleven then. And imagine Isabel actually trying to run from me. Can you believe that?"

I laughed, imagining short-legged Isabel trying to jump a ditch, and Mother on the shoulder of the road, her eyes popping.

Mother turned to me, fork in the air. "It's not funny, Maggie. Now you remember that."

Then she surprised me. She propped one arm on the back of the swing behind Elizabeth, and said, "Well, happy birthday. I'm glad you don't behave like that Isabel." She was smiling.

Thank you, God, for Isabel, I thought. And for Elizabeth not running when she got caught, and yes, for her having the nerve to try to walk to town.

Mother opened her mouth wide for a big bite. Her eyes looked warm and brown. I licked up my last glob of white icing and leaned against her shoulder. Then I reached my leg across Mother's, and for a second, touched my toe to Elizabeth's foot that was still bobbing up and down.

Gil's Roosters 〜

Gil Spencer listened. He rubbed sleep out of his eyes with the heel of his hand. What woke him, he figured, was the crow of the first rooster—the one at the Morgans' house a quarter of a mile away. He was pretty sure. Gil lifted his head from the pillow and stared out the dark screen as though this would help him hear. Still night outside and no other sound, except soft breathing from Maggie.

It was August, and they were sleeping in chipped iron beds on the sleeping porch. His bed and Maggie's pointed east and west, same as the back porch, and Elizabeth's, on the other side, ran north and south. Sometimes he wished Elizabeth was in the bed closest to him; she wasn't as much of a tattletale as Maggie, and he could sneak out sometimes without fear she'd tell Mother. But he hadn't told anybody he was going to meet Leland Wheat at daybreak in the clearing by the Causeys' house. The Causeys were white tenant farmers and didn't own any land. Still, they complained if people shot near their house.

There! Morgan's rooster, for sure, crowing high with a drawn-out end, like an opera singer straining for a note. Gil stretched his legs, still heavy with sleep. In her bed, Maggie grunted. A low-watt bulb, left on in the bathroom down the hall, put out just enough light so Gil could see her there—covered with a sheet, her hair on the pillow lying in two points, like horns. A devil tattletale. Yesterday she'd told on him when he rode his bike halfway to town. Not a sound came from the opposite bed where Elizabeth lay twisted in a ball, her dark hair tousled. Her bed, Gil realized, ran the same direction as the bathtub, and somebody told him that was good luck. Maybe he should switch his bed around.

Ha! More crowing. The rooster further down the road, by Bird's house, was sounding off. The Morgans' cock crowed back, and the two roosters started up a contest—far and near. Gil rubbed his nose with the sheet. Would he hear the third one, the far-off rooster, Sylvester's?

Across the porch Elizabeth sighed, as though she were either disgusted or contented. Contented, probably. Elizabeth loved to sleep. She could snooze until noon if Mother or Augusta, who cleaned, didn't get her up. Last night for the first time Elizabeth had gone to a baseball game in town with her friends. Acted grown-up. Maggie, she was still a twerp.

Gil kept still, listening. Probably it was about four o'clock. The far-off rooster should soon hit it. Maggie teased him about hearing Sylvester's bird a mile away—said he was making it up. No, he wouldn't pretend. In the New Testament the crowing of a third cock was a bad sign—reminded Peter of his denial of Jesus; but Sylvester's was just showing off, saying if you could hear him, this would be a fine day.

Was that it? Gil pulled at his blue-stripped pajama top, freeing it from the sheet. Maybe, but the sound was faint. He pictured Sylvester's unpainted house, the color of branch water, up near the highway. In the swept yard the skinny red rooster would be parading around, picking up his feet. Gil often saw him when he was riding into town and wondered how such a scrawny bird could make such a racket. "Crow loud," Gil whispered.

"Ur-hu-he-ur," came the far-off raucous call, as if the rooster had heard him. Morgan's rooster and Bird's crowed back. Right on the money. Gil gave one delicious stretch, then hopped out of bed. His toes felt the early morning coolness of the floor. In the stillness he lifted his clothes, draped over the foot of the bed—same pants, the same shirt, and tennis shoes he'd taken off last night. All three roosters crowing, it would be a good day.

❧

When the woods road became a bumpy path, Gil got off his bike and pushed it with one hand. The Causeys' house was on the Wheats' land, and Gil had about a quarter of a mile further to go than Leland did. He placed his lighted flashlight in the basket so it shone down on the ground, then shouldered his twenty-two rifle. He hadn't brought his shotgun. Hunting out of season seemed more serious with a shotgun, and he knew his father wouldn't buy him any more shells anyway. When the sun came up, he and Leland were going to shoot squirrels in the woods near the Causeys' house. Leland said it didn't matter that squirrel season wasn't in yet. No game warden came back here. Of course, that's what Leland would say. He never worried about trespassing either, or snitching bullets out of his father's hunting jacket.

Only once before had Gil shot anything out of season. Then it was dove, and Leland was with him. The warden didn't catch them, but his papa did. Gave Gil a lecture that made him feel like a criminal. Leland's father never found out. Leland was just lucky; didn't matter if he heard roosters crow or not. He was like a prancing rooster himself. Gil wished he had some of Leland's luck.

A dark tangle of trees lined both sides of the path. Gil knew these woods in the daylight and that made them less spooky now, in the dark before dawn. On his right an owl gave one short whoo, almost like saying hello. Gil reached for the flashlight, beamed it high in the trees, but he couldn't spot the big-eyed bird. In the sky a pale quarter moon hung low, getting ready to disappear. It was about a half-hour before sun-up.

Gil focused the light on the leafy trail and pushed his bicycle. Ahead, something was flickering and glowing. Leland had gotten there first and built a little fire. He always carried matches, and even in the summer, he would drag up twigs and dead branches, bunch them together, and strike a kitchen match on his pants zipper. Gil wouldn't have built a fire himself, but he liked it when Leland did.

Coming closer, Gil switched off the flashlight. The fire was right in the middle of the path, and close to it, Leland lay like a dark lump, his rifle beside him. "Hey, I'm here." Gil kept his voice low. The Causeys' shotgun house was over a football field away—a slanting shadow in the mist—but sound carried. Leland didn't move.

Gil propped the bike against a tree and stood by the burning sticks, hands on hips. Leland's head was resting on his bent arm, and his ruffled-up blond hair gave him an innocent look, more than was true, Gil thought, and gave a low laugh. In the woods, a bird sounded—a high two-note chirping. Gil sucked in his breath, felt the cool air inside his lungs, felt the briskness of the early morning, still dark but hatching daylight. He tapped Leland's tennis shoe with his toe, glad to be in the woods, just the two of them, waiting for sun-up.

"Wake up." Gil poked harder at the foot stretched toward the dying fire. Leland must have walked; no bicycle lay on the ground. His must still be broke. It usually was.

The head raised up. "Gil?"

"Come on. It's going to be a good luck day. I heard Sylvester's rooster crow, a mile away."

Leland scrambled to his feet, grabbed his rifle. "Roosters? We ain't looking for roosters." He kicked sand on the fire. "Let's shoot a rabbit."

"I thought we were after squirrels."

"Yeah, and maybe a weasel or a fox. I've got bullets."

With the pearly light of dawn, Leland shot at a squirrel. He missed and, gripping his rifle, sallied ahead. Gil followed, and together they scouted the scrub pines at the edge of the clearing, keeping a distance from the gray board house. "Gil, get that one," hissed Leland, reloading. They both fired, watched the squirrel scamper away.

"A rabbit! Quick!" Leland pointed, and Gil raised his rifle and fired at a moving blur in the spiny bushes. The blur kept going.

In the tall pines Leland banged away at tree bark, at squirrels that dodged behind saplings. Dragging more bullets from his shirt pocket, he complained that he didn't have a shotgun. Gil stood in red gooseberry bushes, high as his waist, and anchored the rifle stock to his shoulder, letting his eye follow the silver barrel to the sight. He leveled it on a pine branch thirty yards away. He squeezed the trigger and pow! A brown squirrel dropped.

"Right through the head with a twenty-two!" Leland hollered.

"Just winged him." Gil wished he had killed the squirrel. He hated seeing it drag itself to the bushes. He walked over and pushed limbs out of the way, but he couldn't see the wounded squirrel. Well, he had made a fair shot.

The morning came on, a watery sun rising in a gray sky. Leland used his last bullet shooting at a pine cone. Across a plowed field was the Causeys' dark house, and Gil saw a yellow light appear at a rear window. It bobbed toward the front. "Somebody's lit a lantern in there," he said.

"It's old Mr. Causey finally getting up," Leland said. He let his gun point to the ground and tramped into the field. "Lazy. He ought to be out by now, chopping cotton." Leland jumped a furrow. "He'll be out here in a minute, hollering for us to get off his place. Don't matter. We've used up our bullets."

"Think he'll complain?" Gil stepped onto the plowed ground.

"Complaining is his middle name. But not to your papa. To mine." Leland laid his rifle down and lifted a clod of sun-baked dirt. Grinning, he held it out. "Take this, Gil. Take it and hit the side of his house. Get him out here. Give him something to clamor about."

"*You* throw it," Gil said. His insides rippled.

"Think I won't?" Leland tossed the dirt ball into the air, as though warming-up.

Gil stared at the sagging gray porch, pictured Mr. and Mrs. Causey inside. Doing what? Watching them? Or maybe just sitting at an oil-cloth covered table, eating side-meat bacon and grits. He guessed it wouldn't hurt to scare them a little.

Leland wiped his nose on his sleeve. "Just watch my smoke." He ran down a furrow, and a few yards from the house, he pulled back his arm and slung the dirt clod so hard he stumbled.

Glass shattered. Gil heard Leland say, "Oh, damn."

Turning, Leland shot back down the furrow, his mouth half-open, as if Mr. Causey were on his tail. But when he reached Gil, he laughed. "Got a window! Let's go!"

Gil started to say something, then hushed when Leland jerked his arm. They sprinted toward the pines. Behind them, Mr. Causey called, "Stop, you Wheat boy!"

"No way in hell," panted Leland.

In the woods Gil grabbed the handlebars of his bike, still leaning against the sycamore tree. "You gonna have to do something about the window," he said, pedaling hard, his gun balanced in the basket.

Leland was running down the path pretty fast to be carrying a rifle. "He'll cool off." Leland gulped air. "If he starts drinking, he'll forget."

The woods got denser, and Gil slowed, glad to be out of Mr. Causey's sight. "He'll remember when it starts raining in. Mrs. Causey'll know."

"I got four dollars at home." Leland slowed his pace. His blond hair was plastered to his forehead. "I'll pay him. But he'll just spend it on liquor anyhow."

Leland sure knew out to handle things, Gil thought, even though Mr. Causey saw him. That was as good as luck. Better.

"How you know the rooster you heard was a mile away?" asked Leland, trotting beside the bike.

"It's Sylvester's rooster," said Gil, feeling good that Leland remembered. "His house is by the highway, that far."

Leland stopped to throw some rocks at a squirrel scurrying up a tree trunk. Gil wanted to keep moving, and he motioned. "That was the third rooster I heard this morning," he called, barely pedaling. But Leland wasn't listening.

"Missed that sapsucker," groaned Leland as the squirrel zipped out on a limb. He turned to Gil and laughed. "But I didn't miss the Causeys' house, did I?"

They walked on to the Spencers', Gil pushing the bike and Leland toting both rifles.

They ate a huge breakfast, just the two of them at the dining room table with Bird bringing in plenty of toast, then Leland left on Gil's bike to ride to town. Gil let him borrow it. He knew his own mother wouldn't let him ride in today, so he just shrugged when Leland asked.

An hour later, at eleven, the sun was hot. His blue shirt damp with sweat, Gil sat on the shady end of the back porch steps, cleaning his gun. He gave the barrel short hard strokes. Something about Leland leaving on Gil's own bicycle didn't sit right. Why hadn't he said no? Leland was just riding to town to have fun. Gil broke open the rifle and rubbed the rim of the barrel. Leland had said he'd give Mr. Causey the money late in the afternoon. But would that be soon enough? Would four dollars satisfy? Gil shoved the cloth an inch inside the silver barrel and pulled it out. He could walk to Mr. Causey's and give him a dollar and a half, he supposed. Might keep him quiet. But if Leland wasn't worrying, why was he?

In the hall, the phone rang. Gil snapped the gun closed and sat still. Behind him, Maggie picked up the telephone and gave a loud, "Hel-lo." She said something softer that sounded like "Mr. Wheat." Gil curled his lip. Maybe he and Leland had been seen, and now Mr. Wheat wanted to tell Papa. But he shouldn't be sweating this out. Leland busted the window! Leland, who at breakfast had eaten ten pieces of toast! More than Gil could. He gave the gun stock a swipe with the cloth. Why wasn't *he* the one in town, going to a picture show, instead of Leland?

He glanced into the hallway. Maggie was writing on a note pad by the phone. "OK. 'bye," she said and hung up.

"What was that all about?" he called, causal as he could.

Maggie stared through the screen door. "It was for Papa. Why?"

"Was it Mr. Wheat?" Gil twisted around on the step.

"Yes, if you must know. He wanted Papa to call. I left a note, and I wrote it good." Maggie paraded onto the back porch. "Mr. Wheat asked if Leland was here. He sounded mad. Is Leland in trouble? If he is, I bet you are too."

"No, I'm not!"

"If you've done something, you'll get a whipping."

"Shut up." Gil gave the stock a last lick. He better get on to the Causeys. He stalked into the hall, glanced at the note on the telephone table. He could pick it up. Maggie wasn't looking. Better not, he'd get caught. Probably he was as good as caught already. Trouble was, if Mr. Wheat was going to tell on him about the Causeys' window, he *wouldn't* get a whipping—he'd had only one of those in his life, and it hadn't been so bad. Leland would get the whipping; he'd grit his teeth while Mr. Wheat laid it on with a belt, then walk away, rubbing his seat but already thinking about what was for supper. But Gil would have to stand in front of the fireplace while Papa talked low about un-Christian behavior, his eyes looking the other way; then, feeling six years old, listen to Mother lecture on bad companions. He'd have to sit in a chair for an hour. Then he'd hardly be able to eat supper because Mother, at her place, would be silent and cross. Leland had all the luck.

In the hallway Gil brought the gun stock to his shoulder and aimed at a overhead light. Leland was probably standing in line at the ticket booth now, while he was having to hunt up drunk ol' Mr. Causey. Even crowing roosters didn't help him. Gil lowered the rifle, stashed it with the other guns, leaning against the wall in the corner. He was unlucky. He was really stupid!

Gil rummaged in his bureau and found enough change to make up two dollars. That should hold Mr. Causey until Leland got back, and it might help to tell Papa he'd already paid his part.

⌒

Gil had never been on the Causeys' porch before, and he walked carefully. One of the floor boards was missing, and underneath was sandy dirt. The plants growing in lard cans had some brown, wrinkled leaves. The geraniums, especially, made Gil feel kind of sad; his mother would've had them watered and fertilized in a jiffy. Mrs. Causey must be inside because Gil heard some dishes rattling, but before he could knock, Mr. Causey rounded the corner of the house. His shoulders were more slumped than Gil remembered.

Scuffing his feet on the bottom step to get off the dirt, Mr. Causey nodded, as if seeing Gil there didn't surprise him.

Gil felt too uneasy to even say hello. "This is for the window. That's two dollars," he said, holding out a fist of coins. Behind Mr. Causey, the yard looked empty. Gil wished the Causeys at least had a dog or a cat. "Leland is going to pay you two more. Will that be enough for a new glass?"

Mr. Causey reached for the change, gazing at Gil with hazy blue eyes. "You paying for that Wheat boy?"

"He'll pay too, like I said."

"Probably won't," said a voice back in the house. Steps sounded on the board floor. "This ain't the first time he tore up something."

Gil turned. Mrs. Causey walked to the doorway and frowned, shoveling her hands into her apron pockets. She was tall with a long, scrawny neck, and one eye was pink and puffy. It looked like a sty on the lid. He'd had a bad sty once, went to the doctor to get it lanced.

"Hello, Mrs. Causey," Gil managed to say. "Leland'll pay. I'll remind him." He'd never seen her up close. She was bigger than he thought, and on the front of her apron was a faded rooster, of all things, standing proudly by a little brown hen. Embroidered, he guessed. A rooster! For luck?

"You see this red place?" Mrs. Causey pointed to the spot on her right eyelid, where the sty was.

"That's what your friend done. The rock he threw hit the table and smacked up right in my face. Like to put my eye out. Glass everywhere."

"Just one piece," Mr. Causey put in, gripping the change.

"That's terrible," said, Gil, squinting. He wasn't sure if it was a sty or not. "Do you need to see a doctor?"

"Ain't nobody paying for a doctor, I can tell you that. The Wheat boy don't make amends." She turned and stalked away—more like a rooster than a brown hen, Gil thought. Leland's rock probably hadn't hit her eye. Still, it could have, and Mr. Causey might tell. Gil reached into his pants pocket, pulled out a quarter and a nickel, and held them out. "Take this too. And Leland'll be around."

He took the coins. Gil hoped Mr. Causey wouldn't ask if he was the one who was with Leland this morning, and he didn't. Mr. Causey was being polite. He didn't act drunk either.

They talked a minute about the wilting corn crop, Gil trying to think up good questions. Then Mr. Causey asked where he could buy a secondhand radio. Gil didn't know, but leaving, he started to think of places that might sell one. Mr. Causey might rather have that than a new window pane.

At dusk, Gil rolled his bike across the front yard to its usual place. Leland had returned it, told him about the cowboy picture show, and left, saying he'd pay Mr. Causey two more dollars tomorrow, and Mrs. Causey couldn't have been hurt; but she sure knew how to play act.

Gil was mad at himself. He should've demanded his two dollars back before Leland trotted off. No need to mention the extra thirty cents, or how everything at the Causeys' looked like it needed water, or how he felt when he got back and heard his papa talking to Mr. Wheat on the phone, discussing a fence line. A fence line! Not a thing about hunting or the window. In a way Gil was glad he'd given Mr. Causey the money, but when he thought about Leland at the picture show all afternoon, he felt like a big sucker. Leland hadn't done anything but have fun! He made his own luck.

Gil passed a big camellia bush and leaned the bicycle against the side of the house. The front door slammed. Gil saw Maggie, in a white sailor dress, hop down the steps and cross the yard, heading toward the Studebaker. Gil started to call out in a snide voice, "What you up to, smartie?" Instead he stayed behind the big camellia.

Maggie opened the car door and reached in. Gil tiptoed to a smaller bush at the corner of the front porch. Hunkering down, narrowing his eyes, he felt like a spy. Maggie was always so sure of herself, a little stuck-up brat! If she hadn't left the note for Papa, he might not've gone to the Causeys at all. He'd be two dollars richer, and wouldn't have to ask Leland for his money back.

Maggie slammed the car door. It was pretty dark, but Gil could see a book in her hand, some book she'd left in the car. Probably, she'd been to the library—reading, even in summer. Gil stuck out his tongue as though gagging. Maggie thought she was so perfect! Made him sick.

Carrying her book, Maggie prissed across the yard. He should frighten her. If Leland were here, he'd make her jump. She deserved to be scared more than the Causeys. Gil looked down to see if he could find a dirt clod, but the ground was smooth. Well, he'd do something else.

"Uh-a-uh-ah!" he hollered, flapping his arms, half-hidden by the leafy bush. He meant to sound like a gorilla, but the noise was more like a mad rooster. "Uh-ha-u-ha!" he yelled again, not minding what it sounded like. He hopped up and down, rattled leaves with his arms.

Maggie dropped the book. She didn't run, the way Gil thought she would. "Ooh," she finally got out, a weird look on her face.

Gil laughed through the leaves. He cupped his hands so his voice came out funny. "This is a monster telling you to turn around three times. If you don't, you're doomed."

But Maggie sank to the ground.

"Hey, it's only me!" He stuck his head around the bush.

Maggie lay crumpled, her white sailor collar trailing off to one side.

Gil jumped backwards. If he moved fast, he could run down the road, then come home again, pretend he'd just found Maggie, stretched out. Hope she hadn't recognized his voice. Or he could slip around back, sneak in that door. But Maggie looked so still. Did children her age have heart attacks?

"Mother!" shouted Gil.

Moments later, he helped Mother lift Maggie to her feet. She started to cry. "Something awful's in the bushes," Maggie wailed. "A monster!"

"Really?" said Gil, brushing off her white skirt. "What'd it look like?" He kept his eyes down, felt his heart beat in his throat.

"I-I don't know." Maggie held to Mother's arm and breathed in gulps. "But it sounded *bad.*"

Gil gave her arm a pat. Good! She was alive, and she didn't know it was him. He was pretty lucky. And he could shoot too—better than Leland—without seeing a cowboy movie.

"Don't be silly, Maggie," said Mother, smoothing her hair. "Nothing's in the bushes. You just got scared. I think you played too hard this afternoon without eating, but you could be coming down with something. I'm going to take your temperature."

"Maybe you're beginning to hear voices," Gil said.

"Did not hear voices!"

They started to walk, Gil a little behind.

"You know what I heard this morning?" Smiling, Gil pushed his dark hair off his forehead. "Maggie, I heard Sylvester's rooster, a *mile* away."

"No, you didn't," grumbled Maggie, mounting the steps.

"Yeah, I did. Next time, I'll wake you so you'll know it's true. And you know something else? I'm going to beat you into the house!"

"No you won't," said Maggie, speeding up.

"Just watch my smoke," Gil said, using Leland's words. With a push of his heels, he scooted around Maggie and Mother and dashed through the front door.

Division ~

A wide hall ran down the center of our house. Toward the front, a worn green loveseat and chairs formed a low, saggy group, and farther down stood a tall hall tree. Coat knobs surrounded its clear oval mirror. Mother paid little attention to furnishings, even then, but sometimes on the way to the back porch, she would glance in the mirror and touch her hair or pause long enough to run her hand over the smooth dark wood.

During hot weather, we would sit in the hall not far from the tree with Mother, comfortable in the rocker, Maggie on her lap, and me, Elizabeth, hanging on where Maggie left off. The end of the toe, I called it. The double doors at the hall's front end stood open; so did the wide door leading to the back porch. Cool shadows spread around us with light sliding in—smooth, pale yellow. But when the weather changed, we didn't sit in the hall. One of the front doors would be closed, then the other. Only on icy winter days was the back door shut too. Then the hall looked dark and closed in, and the rifles and shotguns stacked behind the back door were visible again. Hunting guns, six or seven. I'd forget about them during the summer; then suddenly there they were, leaning against the wall, their dark, naked barrels pointing at the ceiling. The first sight of them startled me, and I'd think of pioneer days and picture Indians hiding in the woods. But it didn't bother me very long that hunting guns stood in the corner. Papa and Gil liked them.

In early October, we hadn't yet closed the first of the front double doors. Still, on that particular morning the hall felt a little cool, so Maggie and I lounged in the back porch swing, the sun directly on us. We were glad it was Saturday, no school. Maggie was in the third grade, I in the sixth, and Gilbert in high school—eighth, another world. I pushed my foot against the straw rug to give us some movement and listened to Maggie brag about making the **A** honor roll. We'd gotten our report cards the day before, and I'd only made the **B**. We watched Gil, who hadn't made any honor roll and didn't seem to care, pedal out of the yard on his bike. Then Mother's quick footsteps sounded in the hall. She was talking to Papa, whose steps we could hardly hear.

"Do we *have* to mark it, Frank? This really isn't such a fine piece, and it's too tall for any of their houses. You know how much I like it." Mother talked in a loud voice because she claimed Papa's hearing was getting worse. They were standing by the hall tree, I could tell, although we couldn't see them from the swing.

"We *have* to mark it." Papa was talking low. We stopped swinging. He said, "But I'm pretty sure I can work out a swap if Charlie gets it. I'll give him a couple of chairs."

"I doubt Ethel will go for that!" Mother gave a disgusted sigh. I could picture her eyeing Papa, tall beside him even though they were the same height. She wouldn't be looking in the mirror then—probably the back of her head showed in the glass, her brown braids crossing above the nape of her neck. I could almost see the braids. Then we heard her march to the other end of the hall, and it sounded like Papa walked into his room.

"What kind of mark?" Maggie turned to me, her eyes wide.

"You know, like that piece of paper over there. For the dividing up." I pointed to a long, caned bench on the other side of the porch. A blue paper square was taped to the curved wood of its back. The bench was made like four chairs joined together. Mother said it was an unusual piece. "I hope we draw that one."

"Draw? Like a picture?"

"*No*. I thought you were so smart! They told us about dividing the furniture last night."

Maggie fell into a pouty silence, and I pushed hard against the mat with my foot.

At supper, the night before, Mother said in a matter-of-fact voice that when our aunts and uncles drove out on Sunday afternoon, they wouldn't bring their children. Gilbert groaned. He liked showing our cousin Kenneth around the barn and the cowpen. Mother explained that some of the furniture in the house—only the oldest pieces—was going to be divided up. This should have been done after our grandparents died, but it had been put off; now everybody thought it was time. Papa said it was only fair. His brothers had a right to their part of the old things, even if they didn't live in this house anymore. They would draw for turns and choose. There wouldn't be many pieces that would leave, and we might buy some new furniture! Papa said he would tape a blue square on each piece that was up for the choosing.

"You don't have to put up the twelve gauge, do you?" asked Gil in a tense, high-to-low tone. He was small for fourteen, but his voice was changing. Papa said he would hang on to the gun somehow. We wouldn't even miss the other stuff, and he'd already looked at a brown wicker living room suite, only slightly used, more comfortable than what we had.

"Yeah," yelled Maggie. "New chairs!"

I didn't smile. I'd never thought much one way or another about the furniture in the living room—mission oak, Mother called it. Still, I couldn't imagine those lumpy old pieces gone.

Now, Maggie acted as if she'd forgotten what Papa said. She tucked her legs up in the swing, turned her mouth down, and asked who was going to get our furniture and why. I said she was at the supper table, same as me, and last night she'd sounded like a cheerleader when Papa said we would get some new stuff.

I jumped out of the swing, ran to the caned bench, and yanked off the blue paper square. "Go stick this on the shotgun Gil likes. Watch

him have a fit." I wasn't even mad at Gil; I just had a flash of mean-
ness. Then I laughed. "He'll kill you. But maybe there's already one
on it." I stuck the paper back on the seat with the same piece of rumpled
adhesive tape and ran to the other end of the long back porch.

❦

Bird wasn't in the kitchen. I spotted her outside at the wooden table
by the fence, holding onto a squawking, brown chicken. Bird, our
cook, was on the tall side, like Mother. Her white puffy hat covered
every bit of hair, and a growth, the size of a small balloon, pushed
against the left sleeve of her print dress. Last Christmas we gave her
the material for the dress. I'd helped pick it out. We usually gave Bird
flower prints, and Augusta, who cleaned and did the dairy work, ging-
ham checks or stripes.

Bird pressed the struggling chicken flat on the table, lifted a big
knife, and whacked off the head. I heard the blade hit. Red and yellow
stuff spewed out, and the headless body flapped against the boards. I
squinched up my face and kept walking to the table. Bird was calmly
plucking the body, feathers everywhere. Blood streaked down her fingers. Two years ago, Bird got fired. Augusta became our cook for a
while, and then Bird was allowed to come back, and we were glad.
Her drinking was better, Papa said.

I asked her if she didn't hate to cut off a chicken's head. "Huh," she
said, taking it like a joke, "you like the pulley bone, don't you?"

I nodded. Last Sunday Maggie and I pulled one apart. Maggie got
to make the wish.

Bird held the chicken up and brushed away feathers. "Can't wring a
chicken's neck 'cause God told us not to. Don't eat things strangled in
their own blood. That's what your mama say." She laughed, putting
the back of her hand in front of her mouth to cover her bad teeth.
Bird would laugh about most anything, except Mother firing her. But
in spite of that happening the way it did, she and Mother were still
friends.

"That chicken's a mess, and so's the table," I said. "It's wobbly, and
look at the scarred places where you've chopped down." I touched a
pool of dark blood near the scrawny severed head. The knife lay be-

side it; specks of wood and some stringy, yellowish gunk stuck to the red-stained blade. "Yuk!" I said.

"Killed many a one here. Sure have." Bird threw a handful of feathers on the dark, hacked-up boards.

"At least this old piece doesn't have a blue paper stuck on it." I leaned against the table. It was shaky.

"Nobody'd want this old thing. I use it, that's all."

We talked, and Bird acted like dividing the furniture didn't amount to much. Said Papa would manage things fine. I thought of Mother and the hall tree. If she asked for something, she expected it, and what if Papa couldn't make a swap? But I didn't want to talk about that. "Suppose somebody gets the shotgun Gil likes," I said instead. That would get Bird's attention. She was crazy about Gil.

She stopped plucking. "Gil's gun? No, he wouldn't like that! Tell your Papa to leave those guns behind the door. Just don't shut it. Nobody see them."

"He might have to bring them out. Those that work anyway, and the twelve gauge is one."

"They don't need to divide them guns. No. Yo' Uncle Charlie, he shoots dove now and then, but he can buy his own self a fine new shotgun."

"It's not really Gil's gun; it's Papa's. Maybe his brothers' too, I don't know. But Papa doesn't hunt much anymore." I lifted a feather, touched the blood-stained tip.

Bird went back to plucking. Suddenly I asked, "Are we poor, Bird, do you think? I heard Mother say we were."

"Poor? No sir. You got plenty of food, pretty clothes, and nice sheets on your bed. Your granddaddy bought them sheets in New York City. Don't think you poor 'cause you losing a stick of furniture."

I started to ask her about the sheets coming from New York City, but I didn't. Whatever place they came from, it must have been a long time ago. Last week I'd seen Mother sew two split sheets together. She took the best part of both and made another sheet with a ridge down the middle.

"Don't let nobody see behind the hall door," Bird said, holding up the headless, plucked chicken by the legs. It looked so naked and ruined that I didn't want to eat any of it, not even the pulley bone piece.

C~

In church, Maggie and I sat between Mother and Papa. Uncle Leon
and Aunt Ruth were in the pew in front, and Gil was sitting somewhere with his friends. Maggie leaned her head against Mother's shoulder, and I edged close to Papa. Things seemed peaceful, as though
nobody was worried. But I said a prayer. I asked God to let us keep
everything—on the porch and in the hall and in the living room.

Two things in church I liked: what Papa did when somebody was
praying at the front—he'd get down on one knee between the pews,
bow, and put his head in his hand, as though he were really in front of
God—and I liked to hear Mother sing. Her voice sounded clear and
strong, and she sang on key. She believed the words, I could tell. In
our church we never used pianos or musical instruments, but with
Mother singing, you didn't miss them.

"Oh, thy fount of every bless-ing, tune my heart to sing thy praise,"
she sang, moving the songbook up and down in rhythm. "Streams of
mer-cy, never ceasing, call for songs of loudest praise."

Maggie nestled in, peering up in Mother's face, trying to sing just
like her. Mother didn't have to look down at the words. She knew
every verse.

That afternoon I leaned against an oak tree in the front yard and
watched Rose, Maggie's friend, climb out of a dark sedan. Rose waved
at Maggie, coming down the front steps, while Mother stood by the
car and talked to Mrs. Belote. I could tell by what they were saying
that Maggie had called Rose and invited her to our house without
Mother knowing.

"We'll manage, Mrs. Belote. Don't worry. Maggie and Rose can play
in the back yard, just not around the house." Mother glanced down
the road at a car rounding the curve. "Excuse me, please. I've got to
greet my kinfolks."

Maggie and Rose ran around the side of the house, and I wandered
toward Mother. Mrs. Belote circled the large dirt oval and was heading out as the green Chevrolet with Uncle Leon and Aunt Ruth rolled
in. They stopped beside our blue Studebaker. Right behind, as if they'd
intentionally formed a procession, came a long black Buick with Uncle
Emory looking tall at the wheel and Aunt Mamie scrunched down

beside him; then a pick-up truck with Uncle Charlie and large Aunt Ethel, both sitting straight in their seats. "Do you think they brought their truck so they could haul stuff?" I whispered.

"No!" Mother said, as if I'd asked something wrong. The aunts and uncles were all getting out, and she hurried toward the cars.

"Hello, hello," said Uncle Leon, his voice like a bullfrog. "Didn't know we were in a caravan." He was taller than Papa, with a reddish outdoors face, and he had on a short-sleeved white shirt. Laughing, he took Mother's hand, turned, and said, "Hey, sweetheart," to me. I raised the corners of my mouth in a pretend smile. They chatted, all mixed together like worms in a can. They acted as if this were just any Sunday afternoon. But I saw Aunt Ethel peep over my shoulder at the house and tug at her skirt, straightening it, as though she were getting ready to rush in and choose.

A few minutes later, I sat down in a chair on the shady side of our playhouse. The house was mossy green with SPIRIT OF SOUTH GEORGIA painted in white across the boards above the tiny front porch. The white paint was getting dim. Nobody called it by its name anymore except Mother once in a while. She would smile and look pretty when she said it. She'd named the playhouse herself, she told us, when it was built—a year or so after Lindbergh's flight. She'd taken the name of his plane, the Spirit of St. Louis, and changed it to suit us. Back then, I was told the playhouse was mine; Maggie was just a baby, and Gil wasn't interested. He liked the woods better. Now, we just called it the playhouse, and nobody but me seemed to remember it was mine.

I tilted back in my chair and watched Maggie and Rose play their silly game of trapping chickens. They never knew what to do with the things once they caught them. They'd laugh and holler, then let the chicken go. Rose was sprinkling corn in a trail leading to a shallow trough they'd dug, not far from where I sat. The kernels looked as yellow as the sun against the gray dirt. Rose's hair was a paler yellow, and she wore it in ringlets. I knew Maggie envied her hair. Maggie's was light brown and straight with a Dutch-boy cut.

Rose's curls and Maggie's bangs almost touched as they rationed

out the corn. "Here comes a hen," yelled Maggie. "A Rhode Island
Red! I'll hide behind the playhouse. Finish the trail up to the trough,
and I'll jump out and grab her." Rose did what Maggie said. It worked!
"Eeek!" screamed Maggie. She held onto one leg and kept the thrashing chicken away from her body. "You got her, you got her!" called
Rose. But she drew back from the beak and flapping wings. The hen
squawked loud. Maggie let go of the legs, and they chased the chicken
across the yard.

In a minute they began scattering more corn, yet Rose kept lifting
her head, eyeing the house. I stared too. On the porch Uncle Emory
ran his hand along the back of the caned bench. Aunt Ethel peered
out the screen door, then whipped around and walked toward the living room. It would've been like a normal visit if they'd just sat down.

"What are they doing in there?" Rose asked, raising her lip. "They
act like they're looking for something."

Maggie tossed a few yellow kernels and said in a put-on voice,
"They're dividing up our furniture. We might not have anything left."

"Really?" Rose's eyes rounded. "Won't you get to keep some?"

"Of course we will," I interrupted. "Maggie, you don't tell it right.
It's just some *old* pieces."

"Well! Mother wants the hall tree, but somebody else might draw
it, and Gil thinks they'll get his gun."

"We'll have plenty," I said. Inside, two figures roamed the hall. I
drew a deep breath.

"Maggie, will somebody get the picture you brought to school?"
asked Rose. She'd lost all interest in chickens, and stood with a hand
on her hip, eyes narrowed. Rose was a gossip, I thought. Maggie said
that at school Rose had covered her notebook with all the boy-girl
pluses, making up half of them, like Maggie + Joe.

"What picture?" Maggie glanced up. Then it dawned on her. "Oh,
the one that changes!" She turned to me, her face crinkling up. "They
won't take that, will they, Elizabeth?"

I didn't know. Surely someone would want the picture hanging over
the living room door. When you looked straight-on, there was the
head of George Washington with fine vertical lines on the surface you
could barely see; move to the right, the face changed to Thomas
Jefferson, to the left, James Madison. Those lines made it do that,
brought out a new man. People liked to look at Washington, then

walk from one side of the other, and say "Ahhh," when the face changed. That's why Maggie took the picture to school, to show off the different faces. Finally, I said to Maggie, "I don't think so. But Gil might sure enough lose his gun." I didn't want to talk about Mother's hall tree in front of Rose.

Maggie smiled as though I had solved everything. If someone had to have bad luck it might as well be Gil, she seemed to agree. She pushed Rose into another game, hopping from one spot of shade to another, and trying to reach the fence without getting in the sun.

I ambled toward the house and stopped on the side of the steps— not touching the porch—and through the window I could see the heads in the living room. They'd finished poking around and stood all bunched together near the fireplace.

"A-ha, I got number one." Uncle Leon's throaty voice came through the window. "Ruth, honey, you do the picking. Now, Edith, you say so if you feel uncomfortable and want to leave. I know you're used to things as they are."

"No, it's all right," Mother said in a too-high voice. "This is fair, and it has to be done."

I tiptoed. Papa was passing a plate to his brothers so they could drop a piece of paper back on it. They'd just drawn for turns. Next they would choose. Had Papa drawn too, or did we only get what was left?

Aunt Ruth seemed to be touching a little table in the corner, one I never noticed much. She nodded. Then Aunt Ethel moved toward the piano and turned a rocker on its side to examine it underneath. Her back in a lavender-flowered dress looked broad and strong, as though she could carry that chair out of the house with one hand. But she shook her head. Mother, in a brown-and-white dress with pearls, her church clothes, was resting her folded hands on the back of a mission oak chair, watching the others. Uncle Emory stood in front of the door, gazing up; his long, tilted nose seemed to be pointing at something, like a hunting dog spotting quail. Maggie's picture. Would he choose it? Near the window, Aunt Mamie ran her thin, speckled fingers over the back of a straight chair. Her glasses glinted.

Aunt Ethel, my loudest aunt, boomed, "Let's go into the hall. Come on, Charlie."

I stepped sideways toward the covered well, where they wouldn't spot me but I could see them—white shirts on the uncles' sloping shoulders, prints on the aunts' rounded ones. Suddenly I wanted to punch each one. I said to myself, Go ahead, take it all, look behind the door. I don't care. Take the twelve gauge. Take the hall tree too. They drifted to the left, where the hall tree stood. I pictured Mother wrinkling her forehead, her eyes brown and sad. "No, take Gil's gun instead," I said aloud. They angled toward the corner, as though they'd heard me. Somebody was swinging the back door closed! Then I couldn't see anything at all.

I ran. I wanted to get away from the house where my aunts and uncles, like outsiders, were changing everything. I flew past the garden, past a grape arbor, and slowed down at the first building—a big gray storage barn that held picked cotton, waiting to be ginned. I stopped. The tall wooden door wasn't locked. I'd been inside plenty of times, had run my fingers through the cotton bolls, felt the smooth seed sticking to the fibers. But I'd never been in there alone.

I slid the heavy door open just a crack. Cotton was all over the floor, up as high as the third step of the wooden stairs that ran up one side. The room looked huge and dim, and it had a closed-up cottony smell that made me want to sneeze. But I didn't. Instead, I pushed the door further open, and light came in. The cotton got whiter. We children had often made tunnels here when Papa wasn't looking. Tunnels could collapse and suffocate us, he had warned. Something else we liked was to jump from the steps into the white fluff—that was forbidden too. Jumping packed the cotton down, making it harder to gin, he said.

I quickly climbed the stairs to the sixth step, above the white sea, and did what I wasn't supposed to do. Jumped. My feet hit the stuff, my breath puffed out of me. I fell to my side and rolled. White fibers speckled my corduroy pants. I didn't care. One step higher on the stairs, I stopped, spread out my arms like an angel, and flew down. Whomp. It felt good. I ran up again.

"What do you think you're doing?" someone said in a sassy voice. It was Gil, one foot propped on the door sill. "You're going to get caught. You got it all over you."

I stared at Gil and felt caught already. But I didn't tell him my mean thoughts might have cost him his gun. Instead I stuck out my chin. "I don't care. Just watch." I sped up the stairs, a step higher. Wham! My seat hit the cotton.

Gil laughed, and his dark hair spilled over his forehead. "Go higher!"

I was surprised to hear him laugh. But it sounded good. I hadn't really wanted them to close the back door. "OK," I shouted, and ran up another step. "Ye-ah," I bellowed out and whomped down into the cotton.

Gil joined in. We leaped out as far as we could, yelling when we hit. White flecks flew into the air, stuck to our clothes. We climbed the stairs and jumped from the very top step, hollering loud, glad no one could hear.

Later, on the way to church, nobody talked much. Papa turned on the lights of our blue Studebaker as we reached the highway. It was getting dark. In the front, Mother looked straight ahead. In the back, Maggie told Rose a funny story about picking up the wrong lunch box from the cloakroom at school and finding it had a pig's foot inside. But Rose just sat, solemn and still. I think she knew we were being careful around Mother. Her own mother was always so smiling and sweet that she probably wasn't used to mamas who got mad. When we dropped Rose off, she said, "good-night," and that was all.

In church I beat Maggie to the place beside Mother. Gil sat on our pew for a change, way at the end, swinging his foot in a contented way. His gun was still at home behind the door. The only one that had been taken was an old eighteen gauge he never used. In a way I felt relieved. He didn't know how close he'd come to losing the twelve gauge. Papa had traded a couple of chairs to Uncle Charlie for the gun, which Papa said was a good deal since that make of Ithaca shotgun was rare. "Two perfectly fine caned-bottom straight chairs for a gun, and nothing for the hall tree," Mother said, after it was all over, after the aunts and uncles had ridden off, and we straggled in from outside, white flecks all over Gil and me that nobody even noticed. Mother was standing in the middle of the hall, tense as a drawn bow string. Papa's gray hair looked rumpled, and his eyebrows were pulled together. Ethel wasn't going to let go of the hall tree, no matter if he'd had ten chairs to trade, he explained. Took her awhile to make up her mind, Papa said, but once she had, that was it. But Mother went stalking off. Then Maggie, not paying attention to anybody but herself, burst out crying about the picture that changed. Uncle Emory had chosen it. Papa smiled and said the picture would stay right where it was, over the living room door, for a long time. Emory didn't want it just yet. In fact the only thing leaving soon were the mission oak pieces in the living room—Uncle Leon's now—and Papa had already paid some on the brown wicker set. He poked Maggie in the ribs, and she started to giggle. Maggie was fickle.

From the end of the pew, Gil cut his eyes at me and smirked, which meant he was glad we'd gotten away with jumping in the cotton. I just lifted one corner of my mouth.

When the song leader announced a hymn number and asked us to stand, I leaned toward Mother. She didn't push me away or pull me close. She just looked ahead and sang in her ringing soprano: "Must Je-sus bear the cross a-lone, and all the world go free?" She didn't move the hymn book up and down in rhythm. "No, there's a cross for ev-ery one, and there's a cross for me."

I ran my hand along her arm. I'd felt guilty about wishing Gil's gun away. But right then, if I could have traded it for the hall tree, I would have.

One thing Papa was wrong about. The hall tree left quickly, on Tuesday, the same day as the living room mission oak. But on Wednesday, when he paid for the used wicker set, he found another hall tree—one he couldn't afford, he said, but he bought it anyway. When he moved the heavy piece in, Maggie and I were surprised at how nice it looked— bigger than the other one, with a square mirror and a short bench seat by the place where you put umbrellas. It was a light brown—walnut, he said—and had once been on an estate on St. Simons Island and the wood had only a few nicks. It covered more of the splotches on the wallpaper than our old one had and filled the space good.

But Mother didn't give this hall tree any notice, not the day Papa brought it in and set it up, or the next day. She passed by, not turning or touching the wood. For the rest of the week I waited for her to look into the square mirror and straighten her hair. I wished she'd do it in front of Papa. But she didn't.

On Sunday afternoon, nobody came to our house but Kenneth, who went straight into the woods with Gil. Maggie was in town at Rose's. The weather was even warmer than the Sunday before, the sun bright as a yellow crayon. I was glad to get outside. Bird hadn't come to work that morning, first time she'd missed in months. At breakfast Mother frowned as she served lumpy oatmeal. She said she guessed Bird was drinking again. "I should have known Bird couldn't keep her promise long," she had sniffed.

I sat on the porch of the playhouse awhile, then roamed to the table where Bird whacked off chicken heads. It was so shaky I couldn't sit on it anymore. A leg was folding in. If it wasn't propped straight, the table would soon be tilting to the ground. Bending, I grabbed the crooked leg and tugged. The wood was rotten and stuck an inch into the ground, but I *had* to fix it. This one table that had always been here just couldn't cave in. Bird needed a place to cut off chicken heads. I pulled harder and the leg moved. Another tug almost straightened it. I stood and dusted the dirt and wood slivers off my hands. The table looked a little steadier, but nothing I could do would really fix it. Another leg was beginning to lean. Probably the table would wobble again soon. Fall down. I breathed deep, but the air didn't fill me.

Still, the sun was bright. The branches of the big oaks by the playhouse cast pretty shadows across the swept, cool dirt of the yard, and I began playing Maggie's game—hopping from one spot of shade to another. I made it from the fence by Bird's rotting table to the other side of the playhouse and back, then did it again, taking long jumps to reach the shady spots. This was our yard.

Stone Deaf ~

Sometimes I hated to play with Gwen, our cousin, not because of her hearing problem, either.

"Tell Gwen to turn around, come back this way," our fat aunt Ethel hollered from the bench beside the lake. "She's getting out too far."

We were playing Blind Gator, kind of like Blindman's Bluff in the water. We stopped our game in its wet tracks. "Gw-en," my older sister Elizabeth sang out. She splashed water to draw attention, but Gwen didn't turn. Gwen was watching our other cousin, Kenneth, who was "it" and out a ways, even with the end of the little dock.

"You try, Maggie," Aunt Ethel yelled at me.

Gwen was only to her shoulders in the brown lake water, which, I thought, made it silly to call her in. Gwen was young, almost seven, an only child, and deaf. (Not quite stone deaf, Mother reminded us, although she seemed that way to me.) Mother said all this was why Aunt Ethel hollered so. Aunt Ethel also had a big chest with plenty of lungs.

I scooted water hard and screamed as loud as Aunt Ethel, "Look here!" Gwen turned, her yellow hair slicked back from her round face.

"Out too far," I mouthed for her to lip-read, and rolled my eyes toward her mother. Gwen minded her mother, too much.

"Aw-right," said Gwen, leaning forward and pushing herself toward the shore.

Kenneth, who was nine, my age, went on thrashing his skinny arms through the water, trying to tag us, his eyes squeezed closed. On the bench, Aunt Ethel fanned the August gnats with a white untanned hand. She had driven us to the lake, but she never went in herself. We'd have snickered if big Aunt Ethel had ever put on a bathing suit, but never to her face. I'd as soon snicker aloud at a tiger.

Kenneth tagged me, then I tagged Gwen. When she was "it," we usually let her peep a little since she couldn't hear us splashing. Eyes slit, Gwen lunged at us and missed. Elizabeth, who was twelve, came in close to let herself get caught. Suddenly I could see every bit of Gwen's grayish pupils, the water standing on her pale lashes. "She's looking all the way," I cried.

Kenneth said, "She's cheating!" We splashed her.

"No chee," Gwen claimed, sinking to her shoulders in the water. Gwen talked from the back of her mouth and you had to get used to the way she said things. "I not cheeing."

"Yes, you were," we all cried, splashing her again.

Aunt Ethel hopped up, pumping her arms so that rolls of fat wiggled. "Stop that! You know she can't hear."

"Gwen knows she's not supposed to just look," Kenneth called bravely, then ducked.

"Give her another turn," boomed Aunt Ethel at the edge of the tea-colored lake, "or you'll *all* have to get out."

Gwen stood up, knee-deep in water, and gave a smug little smile. She had on a new white latex bathing suit, one I would have liked myself, and that made her smirky smile harder to take. Kenneth, Elizabeth, and I froze, thigh-deep in the lake. Then Gwen blinked her eyes sheepishly, and said, "I won't loo' next time, but I no wan to be 'it.'"

Aunt Ethel sat back down, but the game was over. We switched to diving off the dock. Climbing up the rickety ladder, I ripped the skirt of my faded cotton suit on a nail so that it hung down and dripped water on my leg like a trickling faucet. It made me feel crabby and tacky. I was glad when we changed into our clothes.

Later, riding into town in Aunt Ethel's sedan, Gwen twisted around in the front seat and said, "Need a new bath suit, Ma-bie." Gwen couldn't say Maggie, my name, very well.

"I'll get one," I sang out, although I felt embarrassed, trapped between Elizabeth and Kenneth in the back seat with nowhere to go. It would be next summer before Mother thought about a new suit for me; then I doubted it would be latex. Aunt Ethel glanced over her shoulder, hands on the wheel, and told us about the deaf school in St. Augustine where Gwen was going for a session. Gwen was wearing a cute seersucker sunsuit I had never seen before. I figured Aunt Ethel would buy her more clothes just to go to that stupid school.

"I'm getting sick of Gwen," I whispered to Elizabeth. "I'm going to get her one of these days when Aunt Ethel's not around."

"Un-huh!" Kenneth grinned as though he hoped I would.

"Oh, Gwen doesn't mean anything," Elizabeth said, her wet brown hair plastered to her small head. Elizabeth thought her head was pointy looking, and that it showed particularly when her hair was wet. It wasn't, but I said anyway, "Your head looks awfully pointy right now."

After Labor Day, school started. We lived four miles from town and every morning Papa drove Elizabeth and me and our older brother, Gil, to our separate brick buildings. Elizabeth and I loved school, and Gil tolerated it without much complaining. Gwen was off in St. Augustine, doing whatever they do at deaf schools. On Sunday afternoons, Kenneth or some friends would come out and we played under the shady oaks in our big back yard. Gil pushed us in the tire swing.

Then, at breakfast one November morning, the day before Gwen was to come home, the tree nearest our back steps with the tire swing— the widest-branched oak of all—fell. It just keeled over, like a soldier at attention fainting from the sun. It wasn't even windy. We heard a great whoosh, then *ka-bang*.

Papa stopped eating his curd; his face went funny. "What was that?" Gil asked, his brown eyes wide. Mother's spoon stopped in mid-air. Elizabeth groaned, "Something big just hit the ground."

We all ran to the back yard. "Tree fell, tree fell!" we hollered, amazed at the change. The bushy oak lay stretched toward the smokehouse, taking up all the yard, branches everywhere, leaves right up to the back steps.

Gil and Elizabeth and I hopped all over the small limbs and climbed onto the big ones. "Gwen's coming out on Sunday. Where'll we play with these branches everywhere?" Elizabeth asked, but Papa didn't hear. It was as though the tree had filled his mind as well as the yard. He had deep furrows in his forehead and several times he said, "I'm sure glad it didn't fall toward the house." He usually worried that a fire would burn us out. Sometimes at night, driving home from church, he'd check the sky for an orange glow out our way. Other times he talked about lightning strikes. I doubt he ever worried about a tree crashing into the roof. Now one had just missed.

We left for school, Mother driving for a change. Papa hired two men to spend all day cleaning, carrying off limbs.

By the next day, Saturday, all the leaves and small branches were gone. The thick trunk sat, upended, its snaky roots caked with dirt. During the morning, the men sawed the thickest limbs into sections so we could burn them in the fireplace come winter. On some nights, we were already building fires.

Elizabeth and I watched the men haul the logs to the woodpile, their dark muscles straining, and we rolled the patched-up tire that used to be a swing back and forth in the cleared places. No more tire swings from that tree, I realized. Papa said the oak fell because it had rotted inside; wind had nothing to do with it. I couldn't get over how easily it had happened. "I didn't know big trees just fell," I kept saying. It left a gaping space overhead. Where there used to be branches, now was only bare sky, a hole in the universe. Our back yard looked naked.

Elizabeth didn't seem to mind that the tree had collapsed and would never again hold a swing. "This is fun!" she yelled, standing on a log. It was early afternoon and the men were gone for the day, leaving some of the thickest sections scattered across the yard. Elizabeth took some shuffling steps and made the log move. "Look, Maggie, I'm log rolling, just like in the picture show."

"I can too," I yelled, taking a giant step to the top of one. We'd seen a western at the Palace where men rolled logs in a river.

At first we inched along, hopping off when we lost our balance. Once or twice we fell. After practicing, we could guide our logs some. "I'm good!" said Elizabeth, rolling past me. She'd picked a log with smooth bark and it moved pretty fast. "We can do it again tomorrow after church."

My log had a bump on it. I rolled a foot and was jarred off. "Not for long," I said. "Gwen's back from St. Augustine, remember? She won't be able to do this."

Elizabeth stopped and frowned. "Can't she try?"

"Aunt Ethel will be on the porch," I said, making a face. "If Gwen falls, you know what." We both groaned. We kept rolling and before we stopped, I'd changed my mind. "Gwen ought to learn how to roll," I said. "We'll do it where Aunt Ethel can't see."

ᢍ

In church Gwen sat at her usual place in the pew in front of us, sandwiched between thin Uncle Charlie on the end and Aunt Ethel. Gwen's blond hair was pulled back with a barrette so that her fair-skinned cheeks showed. She was kind of pretty, I grudgingly admitted.

Aunt Ethel had the fox fur neckpiece she wore on cool days around her full shoulders, and a furry tail dribbled down her back when we stood for a hymn. "Sweet hour of pray-er, sweet hour of prayer," we sang. Aunt Ethel's rich alto blended with my mother's clear soprano, their voices wrapping all around us. The singing made me feel good. Gwen glanced my way. I wiggled my fingers, and she smiled.

Mother saw and gave me a little pat. She liked Gwen. Sometimes she compared us, unfairly I thought. "Gwen may have a ninety percent hearing loss," Mother often said, "but she tries to mind. And you, Maggie, with perfect hearing, don't listen to a thing."

During the prayer, I did something that Elizabeth and I had done before—pretended to bow my head but really leaned forward to get a good look at the brown tails and tiny feet hanging from Aunt Ethel's shoulders. The neckpiece was fancy-looking but weird. It had lots of dangling parts. Elizabeth and I had never been able to decide if it was one fox, split up, or two. One, I thought, getting close. A small pointed head sat on Aunt Ethel's shoulder, its teeth snapping down on its own tail. The hard little glass eyes stared up. I was about to touch the fox's nose, just to prove I could, when the prayer ended.

Gwen turned in her seat. Her plain dress had an embroidered collar that made it almost a party dress. "This afternoon, I come play," she said too loud to Elizabeth, sitting behind her.

"Shuss," Aunt Ethel hissed over her shoulder, aiming her warning at us instead of Gwen.

Elizabeth and I exchanged looks, rolled our eyes. "Grrr," I said low. Then I pointed at Aunt Ethel's neckpiece and whispered, "One fox." Elizabeth smiled, shook her head, and mouthed, "Two."

ᐁ

That afternoon, Elizabeth and I grinned when Aunt Ethel and Uncle Charlie, standing in the hall, said they'd just leave Gwen and come back later. They were going to a reception where children weren't allowed. Aunt Ethel talked on while Uncle Charlie gazed out at the remaining logs and the stump in the back yard. "Used to climb that tree when I was a boy," he mused. "It was old then. Guess it had to go." Aunt Ethel gave us a sweet and threatening look. Her eyes made me think of the fox. "You girls be careful now," she said. "You can play paper dolls."

"Bye, Mauwa," Gwen said, stepping quickly away from Aunt Ethel as though eager for her parents to leave. Gwen still had a little baby fat around her waist and she wore a fuzzy red sweater that made her look even chubbier. The sweater was darling, with a yarn picture of a black poodle on the front, the very same sweater I'd seen at Churchwell's. I'd begged my mother to charge it. "No, Maggie," she had said, looking at me hard. "Seven dollars is far too much. Anyway, for someone so young, you think too much about clothes. Remember: 'Pretty is as pretty does.'"

In the hall, I touched the poodle on Gwen's sweater. "Doggie-doggie. Too nice to play in," I said. Elizabeth gave me a "watch-it" look— almost an Aunt Ethel look.

"Let's pway in the yard," said Gwen, not paying attention to what I'd said. She actually liked Elizabeth and me, even when we teased her.

Mother led us to the back porch and told us to be careful. Then she headed for the garden, never mentioning the logs. When no aunts and uncles were visiting, she gave herself permission to work in the flower beds even though it was Sunday. No one was supposed to work on Sunday since it was God's day. The men in our family didn't even go fishing. Mother did lots at church—taught Sunday School, started a Bible class at the colored church on Grady Street; still she allowed herself to pull weeds on Sunday if she wanted to. I liked the way my mother was, except for not buying sweaters.

Walking down the steps, I was struck again by the big hole in the sky where the branches had been. There was blue, blue, everywhere—too much. The hole seemed to leave us open to the very eye of God. To push away the scary feeling, I said, "We'll show you how to log roll, Gwen." A perfect time for it, I thought. Mother was in the garden, Papa was off somewhere, and even Bird, our cook, had left.

"*I'll* show her after while," said Elizabeth, skipping ahead on her thin legs as if she owned the yard. "Let's do something easy first. Hop-scotch."

"She can't do that very good either," I said pretty loud. "Let's go ahead and roll."

"We'll have to be careful. She can't hear us tell her how."

"Can't hear? That's news to me!" I squinched up my face. Elizabeth was acting like Aunt Ethel. "She can *see*, can't she?" I hopped on a thick log and did a pushing step so that it inched along. "See, Gwen?" I screamed as though I could make her hear. "LOG ROLLING." I shuffled the log toward Elizabeth who stood by the stump, arms folded, a put-out expression on her face.

"Look, nobody's here but us," I said softly to Elizabeth. "Big trees don't fall every day. Get a log." I forgot about God looking down through the hole.

Elizabeth let go a smile. Aunt Ethel wasn't around, so Gwen wouldn't do any smirking this afternoon. And we could actually help her learn something new.

"Watch," hollered Elizabeth, hopping on a log. She shuffled, and it scooted in a semi-circle. "It's eas-y."

"Can't," said Gwen on the steps. She had on black patent Mary Jane shoes, and, with the sweater bunching at her waist, she looked like a chubby doll.

"Whee!" we hollered, rolling around, waving our arms for balance. When we fell off, we climbed back on.

Gwen laughed, seeing it was fun, and came down the steps into the yard. "I'll twry," she said, putting one foot up on a small log. About six more were scattered around the yard. Gwen brought up the other foot and stood on the log, arms out, a weak smile on her face.

"Good. Let's get going," I shouted.

Elizabeth stopped her log and jumped off by Gwen who was still balancing on hers, legs shaking. "Now shuffle your feet," Elizabeth said, pursing her mouth like a teacher. I'd seen her do that before— act superior. Made me sick.

Gwen did a funny sliding step, then flailed the air. Elizabeth grabbed her. Wobbling, Gwen regained her balance. "Ooh, I nearly fwall," she said.

"If you start to fall, just hop off," I said, looking right at her so she could read my lips. "Silly!"

Gwen tried a step, then quivered again.

"She's wearing the wrong kind of shoes," stated Elizabeth. "They're slippery."

I said, "Gwen, do it again."

Gwen tried, lost her balance, and toppled down to her knees. Standing up, she rubbed her hands on the poodle part of her sweater.

"Doggie, doggie! Getting dirty!" I cried. "Get up."

"That's OK, Gwen. We fall too," said Elizabeth, and she turned to me. "I'm going in and get her some tennis shoes. Don't let her roll yet." She ran toward the house.

"See, Gwen." I hopped off my log and faced her. "Just jump off when you start to fall. Easier than getting off a bike. Change to that big log there."

"Aw-right." Gwen took a breath and stepped up on a log with rough dark bark, the thickest in the yard. She took a forward step, quivered, then tried another. The log wiggled, but Gwen couldn't get her feet going right.

"Shuffle!" I screamed. "Do something!"

Gwen pushed with a foot. The log moved.

"You're rolling! We'll show Elizabeth," I yelled. "Now push hard. Go in a circle. Do figure eights!" Of course I hadn't done any eights myself.

"I roll," cried Gwen, sticking out her arms and shuffling. The log bumped forward.

"Faster, faster," I urged.

She pushed, poised on top, but her feet couldn't keep up with the turn. "Yee-ah!" Gwen hollered and beat the air. She pitched forward.

As she hit the ground, the moving log caught her on the back of the leg, and I heard a snap, like a twig breaking. Gwen screamed, her chin in the dirt, arms thrown out. One leg was hooked under the log.

Quickly I shoved the log back and pulled at her arm, trying to raise her. I didn't even have time to feel sorry. In my mind Aunt Ethel's voice thundered, "Maggie! What have you done?"

"Stop," said Gwen, twisting so her light hair swept the dirt. "Ooh," she moaned.

"You're not hurt bad," I said, my insides like Jell-O.

Elizabeth slammed out the back door, holding the tennis shoes. "Maggie!" she yelled, running down the steps. "I told you to wait!"

We managed to lift Gwen from the ground. She cried and groaned and wouldn't put any weight on her left leg, so we held her on either side. "It's not hurt bad," I said again.

"Only a little," put in Elizabeth, giving me a mean look. Then she rolled her eyes, and I knew she was hearing Aunt Ethel in her head, too. We lugged Gwen up the steps. "Ooh," she cried, tears streaming. But at least she was holding onto me and Elizabeth, and not acting mad.

In the living room, we stretched Gwen out on the brown wicker sofa, and Elizabeth ran to get the bottle of Vicks. That's what Mother rubbed on everything.

"Hurts," Gwen wailed and pointed to a pinkish knot rising on her shin.

We smeared on the greenish goo, me gently rubbing it just above her white sock and Elizabeth outlining the knot. "This'll fix it," we kept saying. Gwen whimpered, stretched out on her back, her sweater all hiked up, and her slip showing at her stomach. Elizabeth gave me a frightened stare. I shivered. Elizabeth wouldn't tell, I thought, but Aunt Ethel might guess I was the one who had egged Gwen on. My eyes watered. The thought of Aunt Ethel's voice battering me down seemed much worse than any broken leg. At least Gwen herself hadn't heard the leg snap.

I smoothed down the poodle sweater, no longer wishing it were mine, and spread the Vicks thick. "Mother rubs this on us when we feel sick," I said weakly, but I knew it wasn't going to mend a bone.

The back door slammed. Mother must have heard Gwen's moans, and she rushed into the living room.

I let the Vicks bottle fall from my hand. "Gwen's leg may be broken," I said hopelessly. "I heard a snap. Aunt Ethel is going to kill me."

A minute later Mother was on the hall phone. "Ethel, I should have warned them about those logs," she said. "It's my fault." I looked up from the loveseat where I had wilted down. Mother held the black receiver out from her ear, her knuckles smudged with dirt from the garden, and I could hear the thunder in Aunt Ethel's voice. With her free hand, Mother pushed her glasses up the bridge of her nose, shot me a frown—but not too bad a frown, just worried—and hung on. She was wonderful.

Later, hearing Aunt Ethel plowing up the front steps, I ducked behind the big rocker. Elizabeth had vanished.

"Gwen!" Aunt Ethel charged down our hall ahead of Uncle Charlie and flung herself into the living room. "Oh, my ba-by," she cried. Mother said, "She needs a doctor." There were scraping and grunting noises, and I knew Uncle Charlie was lifting Gwen.

I moved and stood by the front door. I had to say something, I guessed, but my mouth felt full of glue.

"Get out the way," Aunt Ethel bellowed, as though I were an inconvenient piece of furniture, one she could talk to. "Gwen's hurt. Clear the way!"

"Aunt Ethel, I'm sorry about Gwen."

"Maggie, you can't play with Gwen again!" She pushed me aside, her rings scraping my shoulder. "You're the one that led her on, I bet, and then you spread that mess all over my child's poor leg. Elizabeth was always sweeter to Gwen than you. You can't play with her anymore. You hear?"

I felt shoved underwater. I did slow somersaults, going down, down.

As Uncle Charlie turned sideways to get Gwen's legs through the front door, she looked at me, not too mean, nothing like a smirk. "Mabie," she said, and raised a hand so I could see the poodle on the dirtsmeared sweater. "I fell, didn't I?" Right then, I would have bought her a new sweater myself, if I'd had the money.

The next Sunday Gwen thumped down the church aisle on crutches. Below her plaid skirt was a bone-white plaster cast. Uncle Charlie was at her elbow, and behind sailed Aunt Ethel, a full-blown dirigible, her posture erect, the fur neckpiece making her shoulders look grand. Uncle Charlie guided Gwen into the pew in front of us, and the crutches clanked against the wood of the seat like oak limbs knocking together.

At home, the logs were gone from our yard, and where the tree trunk had been was a chewed-up place in the ground. Overhead, instead of leafy branches, was the hole God could spy through when He wanted to, I guessed. I think He'd forgotten to look on the day Gwen fell, or maybe He was just waiting to glare down on me when I was alone. I still wasn't used to all that blank sky.

I hadn't seen Gwen since she was carried out of our house. The times Mother had talked to Aunt Ethel on the phone, her voice was tense when they spoke about Gwen's "greenstick" fracture. More wood, it seemed, but anything called "greenstick" couldn't be all that bad.

In the pew in front of me, Aunt Ethel settled back. The fox head on her shoulder pointed in my direction. The little eyes stared meanly, as if they were saying I was bad and could never again play with Gwen. Still, before the first song, I leaned close. Elizabeth sat further down, next to Papa, her feet in new flat-heeled pumps planted on the floor, and she shot me a look that said, "Back away!" But I didn't. Those eyes dared me, and I lightly touched the fox's nose.

Aunt Ethel must have felt it. She glanced sideways, her fat neck wrinkling. "Gwen," she whispered, bending toward her daughter. "There's Ma-bie." She said it just like Gwen did. And she didn't say it like I was an outcast forever.

I raised one finger and wiggled it. Gwen looked pleased. I decided that next summer, if Aunt Ethel let me play with Gwen, when she opened her eyes during Blind Gator I would carefully explain the rules, even though she already knew them. She could put her fingers on my chin, as she'd learned to do, so she could feel the words. We'd figure out a way she could catch somebody without cheating.

Craning my neck, I saw a second fox head on Aunt Ethel's chest. Its teeth gripped another tail, and it looked like a complete head, not a split-down-the-middle one. This head had eyes that were looking the other way, but they seemed nicer, smoother, and darker than the first fox. I poked Elizabeth, who was flipping through the song book. "Two foxes," I whispered.

She stared at the neckpiece. Grinning, she nodded and held up two fingers. "I told you."

We all stood to sing. "We've reached the land of corn and wine and sweet de-liv-erance there is mine, . . . Oh, Beu-lah land, sweet Beu-lah land." Mother's high soprano and Aunt Ethel's full alto wrapped all around us. Even Gwen's monotone and Uncle Charlie's braying bass.

❦

Months later, I had a dream about Gwen.

In the dream, she held out a little tree branch with ordinary oval leaves. "Maggie, what kind of plant is this?" she asked, speaking plainly. She didn't say 'Ma-bie.'

I laughed. In spite of her improved speech she looked the same, the Gwen I could boss around—broad-faced, blond hair growing too low on her forehead, forming in the middle a fuzzy little peak. Actually her hair was thick with all kinds of nice, wiggly waves—prettier hair than mine. "What kind of plant?" I wrinkled my nose and spoke carefully, as though reminding her that she had to read lips. "Silly, that's just part of a regular tree."

"A big tree?" she asked, her eyes trusting me.

A pin shaped like a dog sparkled on her white Peter Pan collar. I wished I had a cute shiny pin.

"Yeah. A huge one." Quick as a flash I yanked off her doggy pin.

"Stop!" She grabbed at her collar. "My pin!"

"Can't hear you," I hollered, and I ran and ran and ran.

Josephine's Room ⤳

The back of our house had wings that stuck out here and there, but the front was balanced, shaped like the bottom half of an **H**. The protruding rooms were spacious, airy, each with a deep bay window looking north over the front yard. In my grandparents' day the room on the west had been a parlor, Bird said, and was fine. I surely don't remember that. Neither does Elizabeth or Gil. We knew it as Josephine's Room, a place for stuff that didn't fit into the other rooms, where Mother pedaled her sewing machine, and Augusta ironed, or sometimes Elizabeth. Next to the back porch, it was the most popular place in the house.

We never knew Josephine. Mother got her from the Children's Home at Naylor before Gil was born, or maybe he was just a baby. Josephine was about fifteen. Nobody could say exactly why Mother brought her home; she had enough help. Our cook Bird said she thought Mother wanted more children, that she was kind of old—about thirty-five—when Gil was born, and afraid she wouldn't have more babies. I'm not sure that's why; it could have been because the preacher asked her to. Anyway, Mother and Josephine didn't get along. Bird seemed positive about that. None of us ever doubted it from the way Mother talked. When Josephine moved out, the only thing she left behind was her name on the room where she'd slept. We kept on calling it after her. The other side room—the other leg of the **H**—was often called Auntie Bea's room because she stayed there one winter. But we didn't use that bedroom much or always call it by its name, the way we did Josephine's Room. As far as Josephine herself, we hardly ever thought of her, except once in a while Elizabeth would tease Mother and call Josephine our adopted sister.

It was March, and the days were mild. The hall doors stood open, both ends. Mother was in a good humor that Saturday morning when she sat down in the rocker to catch the breeze drifting in the front door. I crawled onto her lap, even though I was nearly ten, and Elizabeth piled on too. She'd just turned thirteen, but was small. She straddled Mother's legs. Laughing, Mother jiggled her knees, the way she did when we were little and she was giving us a ride.

"Tell us about Josephine," said Elizabeth, grinning. "She really was our adopted sister, wasn't she?" We knew what Mother would say, but it was fun to see her pucker up her face.

"Pshaw, not! She was not." Mother looked as if she were sucking a lemon. "I didn't want her for a daughter."

"What happened to her?" I asked, lying back on Mother's chest, taking up all the room. We knew the answer to that question as well. We just liked to hear Mother talk when she was mad at somebody besides us. Sometimes she enjoyed it too.

"I heard from the preacher she was in Akron, Ohio. Married. I pity her husband! She was one cantankerous person."

"What'd she do, so bad?" asked Elizabeth.

"Slide off, Elizabeth. My leg's going to sleep." Mother shifted her knees. "You move too, Maggie."

"Did you write to Josephine after she left?" I asked, not moving, a question I'd never thought of before.

Elizabeth put in with another new question. "When she lived here, what did she like to eat?"

"No, I didn't write. She liked fried chicken, only the white meat, and she wanted plenty of it." Mother brushed us off. "Now hush about Josephine. She didn't even live here a year. She didn't like it. The only thing she was interested in were the boys in her Sunday School class."

"Did she ever write you? Send a postcard?" Elizabeth stood up.

"Not a line!" Mother rose from the rocker, put one hand at her hip. "She didn't believe in thank-you's."

"Where'd she go when she left? Whose house? She didn't get married at fifteen," persisted Elizabeth, sinking into the rocker.

"Josephine was only fourteen when she pulled out," said Mother. "Fourteen, I remember."

Elizabeth stared up, eyes wide. "I'm thirteen. She wasn't much older than me."

"Maybe Josephine went to her grandparents'," I chimed in from the floor. "I bet she had a grandmother." That seemed such a marvelous thing to have, especially since we didn't have any live grandparents. All dead. Elizabeth said she could remember one grandmother, but I couldn't. Bird had told us about Papa's mother, and when we talked about her we called her Miss Trudie, the way Bird did. "She must at least have had an aunt," I said with a sigh.

"Not a soul," said Mother. "Josephine was an orphan. She probably went to another home, but don't waste your pity on her. She could look after herself. She was selfish." Walking toward the back door, Mother said, "That's enough about Josephine. I'm going to gather some eggs for the hunt. We have to dye them this afternoon."

"An orphan," I echoed when the back door closed. That exact word had never been mentioned before. A selfish orphan. Mother had never called her selfish either. How could orphans be selfish if they didn't have anything to begin with and were all by themselves?

"What do you think she did that was so selfish? Eat all the chicken?" I didn't move from the floor, and looked up at Elizabeth slouched in the rocker.

"Who knows," said Elizabeth, arching her eyebrows. She let her hands dangle off the chair arms, like a puppet. "But I'm glad I'm not Josephine."

"What do you suppose she looked like?" Looks might give a clue about selfish orphans.

"Oh, I bet she was a fatty with a kind of pouty mouth and blond hair that she tossed around a lot. I bet she wore pink flowered dresses."

"Like your friend Isabel?" I laughed. I couldn't imagine Mother and Isabel living in the same house.

Elizabeth smiled. "Or worse. She might've been like a fourteen-year-old Mae West, with platinum hair and wearing pink satin clothes. Mother can't stand pink."

We hooted. We'd seen Mae West in My Little Chickadee the Saturday before and afterwards we'd tried to talk low and husky, the way she did. "Mae West wouldn't have lasted a week here!" I exclaimed.

"Not a day."

"I wonder if Mother bought Josephine clothes," I said, trying to picture Mother and this selfish orphan in Churchwell's looking at dresses. Maybe they would argue about how much the dress cost, or because Josephine wanted a really fancy one. This was the most I'd ever thought about Josephine.

Suddenly Elizabeth changed her tone. "I bet she wouldn't have thanked Mother if she did buy her a dress. Josephine was ungrateful. Bird said so too." Pausing, she stared at the back screen door that Mother had walked out of. "Do you think we ever act ungrateful?"

At the far end of the hall, the phone rang. Soon Elizabeth was sitting at the telephone table talking to Mary Louise about some party.

I wandered into Josephine's Room. It was so quiet. Sunlight streamed in a south window and lay across an old trunk loaded with patterns and a wicker basket of scraps. This room used to look huge. It still seemed pretty big, in spite of all the stuff—the oak bed in the north corner, where Gil slept in the winter, the three box seats lining the bay windows which held our dead uncle's old trains; the thick sideboard against the east wall (inside, our Aunt Helen's old maroon high-heeled shoes), the long pole that stretched from the top of the sideboard to a tall hat rack, holding the hangers for Elizabeth's and my clothes. In the south corner sat Auntie Bea's writing desk, her letters still in the drawer, then Mother's machine near the west windows, and back of that, the ironing board, the iron upended and the cord connected to a hanging light socket.

I plopped down on the worn green rug, my back to the cold fireplace; once in a while Augusta kindled a fire there in the winter. Before I started to school, I would sit in here every day beside Mother at her Singer. I'd cut out paper dolls or calendar pictures, and we would talk while she pedaled. Nobody came in much because Elizabeth and Gil were in school and Papa was either in town or in the field. Sometimes Bird stuck her head in the door to ask a question, or Augusta might iron for a while, but mostly it was Mother and me. I would cut out anything she asked me to—Octagon soap coupons, squares from scrap material to be used in church quilts. I loved being with her in Josephine's Room. In the afternoons the sun would stream in through the west window just right, touching Mother and then me. We talked, did our work, and never mentioned Josephine.

Today, only one piece of cloth lay beside the sewing machine and the scrap basket was half-empty. Mother must not be sewing as much. I'd spent less time in here lately, but on the Saturday mornings I didn't go into town, I still sat by Mother at her machine, so I knew she sewed some. Now, the room served another purpose; it was the sit-down place. If any of us—usually Gil, maybe Elizabeth—did anything wrong, we had to sit in a straight chair by the fireplace for as long as Mother said. Still, it was a popular place, all of us going in and out. We'd never used the room much at night, except for Gil to sleep, because the light wasn't good—one weak bulb in the same hanging socket where the iron was plugged.

Did all this stuff fill the room when Josephine lived here? If she had many clothes, she must've had a hard time finding a vacant drawer to put them in. What had she done at night? Did she have enough light to read by, or see herself in the mirror so she could comb her fuzzy blond hair? How could she've been selfish if she was stuck in this junky old room without anything that was hers?

Mother didn't even have a snapshot of Josephine. Trying to picture her was like trying to picture a ghost. It made me shiver. I got up and ran out—past Elizabeth, still on the phone in the hall—to the back yard to help Mother find eggs.

We were heading toward the hen house when Elizabeth called from the porch, "Mother! Can I go in town to Mary Louise's tonight? She's having everybody over. . . ."

"No," hollered Mother. "You need to stay home. I'm not driving you in."

"I never get to go anywhere," grumbled Elizabeth.

Later, she didn't come into the kitchen where Mother and I were dyeing eggs, using lots of bright greens and yellows. The church was having a hunt in our front yard tomorrow. Easter was three weeks away, but our church did things like that—kind of off the holiday. Sometimes we sang "Joy to the World" in July.

The night was cool enough to turn on the heater in the bathroom while I bathed. The heater was round, like an electric fan, with heating coils behind a sagging metal screen. Mother called for me to hurry up; Gil was waiting. When I climbed out the tub, I threw my foot over the side in a hurry, and my toe touched the burning-hot metal screen. I yelled. Mother came running. Ungentine was what she used, a thick coat.

I got into bed, still crying, but I must have gone right to sleep. I didn't hear a sound.

Next morning I hobbled to the dining room in a slipper and found Papa and Gil silently eating oatmeal and Mother, her face pinkish, peering at Elizabeth. "What I want to know is how you knew those boys were in the back yard?"

"I didn't *know*," said Elizabeth, twisting in her chair. "Mary Louise just said they might ride out and I went to look. I told you last night."

"Last night?" I asked. "What happened?"

Mother slapped scrambled eggs on my plate, not answering. She kept on scolding Elizabeth and I picked up that she'd caught Elizabeth slipping in the back door about 9:30. She'd been in the yard with two boys who had ridden bicycles from Mary Louise's to our house.

"All that way?" I was truly amazed. "It must have taken an hour!"

"Only thirty-five minutes," murmured Elizabeth.

Mother gave a disgusted snort. "Imagine!"

Bird collected the egg plate and escaped through the swinging door to the kitchen. Gil spooned up oatmeal, shoulders hunched, and Papa looked up from his dish as though he was about to speak to Elizabeth, but Mother kept on. "You must have timed it well," she said, raising both eyebrows. "You sneaked out and there they were. Were you planning on riding to town on one of those bikes?"

"No-oo. I only went out to see if they got here. We talked a minute and then I told them to leave."

"That's not so bad," I put in.

Mother told me to hush.

"Now, Edith," Papa cut in, "let's talk about this later." Forehead wrinkled, he wiped his hands on a white napkin and folded it by his plate. "This is Sunday, remember."

But Mother fussed at Elizabeth some more and would have sent her to Josephine's Room right then, except it was time to leave for church.

"Elizabeth knows how much I do for her," Mother said, talking to the air. She rose from her chair. "Then she acts like this."

On the way to the car, Elizabeth said to me. "It's not fair. They wanted me to go for a ride but I wouldn't, and Mother still acts like I'm the worst thing around."

That afternoon I stood on the front porch, my right foot in a slipper, while Mother waved to the cars rolling onto the dirt oval under the trees. About fourteen children piled out in a hurry, and then the mothers wiggled from the driver's seats. I kept my lips in a line. My foot would keep me from running, and besides that, my only good friend in the Sunday School class wasn't coming. The others were too young, or were just plain drips.

I hopped along with others to the back porch where Mother directed us; she wanted us out of the way while the adults hid colored eggs in the front yard. As I limped through the back door, I heard Papa's voice: "Watch out!" He was hurrying toward the covered brick well where Elizabeth and our cousin Harold were leaning over the side, staring down. Harold held the rope to the bucket in his hand, and at first I thought they were just drawing water. Then Papa, who hardly ever raised his voice, hollered at Harold for knocking an Easter egg into the well with his elbow. He was mad! This meant the well would have to be cleaned out. Frowning, Papa asked Harold what he was doing with an egg; the hunt hadn't even started. "Elizabeth gave it to me," he said with a nervous giggle. Elizabeth wasn't supposed to have any eggs yet. Papa lectured Harold, and Mother whipped out to the back porch long enough to order Elizabeth to Josephine's Room. "Right now! You can't stay out of trouble, can you?" She put one hand on her hip, eyeing Elizabeth, who kept looking toward the playhouse, or anywhere but at her. "What's gotten into you?" Mother asked. "You just don't mind anymore."

Elizabeth said she was sorry about the egg in the well and stared into the sky. She took her time walking up the steps. When she passed me, Elizabeth said, "I'm too big to hunt eggs anyway."

The Sunday School group was on the back steps and heard it all. I was embarrassed. Then Mother yelled from the front yard for us to come on. The eggs were hidden. I peg-legged it down the hall, the last of the bunch, most of us carrying last year's Easter baskets with some of the grassy stuff stringing down the sides.

We lined up on the front steps, me at the end. The girl next to me had a basket as big as a bucket which she'd probably fill, while I'd be lucky to find anything.

Cupping her hands, Mother shouted that one hundred Easter eggs were hidden, and a prize egg too—a beautiful golden egg! The whistle sounded. Everybody but me scattered, and in a second they were poking at leaves, snatching up eggs tucked in tree roots, behind posts. Holding my slippered foot off the ground, I bent to look under the steps. Nothing there. A yellow egg was nestled beside a pillar of the house, but before I could hobble over, a girl named Alice scooped it up. I started after a pink one by a fence post; Fred dove down and shoved it in his basket. I crept back toward the steps, feeling like a lonely cripple.

Someone touched my arm, and I turned to face Mother. She bent down, and the white collar of her brown dress brushed my cheek. Her perfume smelled clean and sweet, like a flower. "Why don't you duck up under the limbs of that big japonica?" she whispered and nodded toward the waxy-green bush by the west bay window. "Nobody's looked there. You can hop that far." I was too surprised to say anything. Then Mother was gone, patrolling the yard.

The bush was really a small, leafy tree. No half-hidden eggs lay at the roots. Disappointed, I grunted and turned my gaze upward. Over my head, in the crook of a branch, something shone—an egg, a bright one. The golden egg! I stretched and carefully brought it down. It was twice the size of a regular egg and heavy in my hand. Mother had actually sent me straight to the golden egg, not just an ordinary pink one, but the *prize*. Underneath the gold paper, I knew, was chocolate! Grinning, hidden from the front yard by leaves, I cradled the egg in both hands.

I turned toward the house and glanced up. There, between the branches, I saw Elizabeth sitting on the window box in Josephine's Room. She looked out at me, kind of smiling. I held up my prize egg! She just kept looking, leaning toward the window, her chin propped on one hand. Elizabeth was sitting so still she seemed frozen. Josephine popped into my mind. Her hair might have been brown, like Elizabeth's, instead of blond. Had Josephine sat like that—not moving, staring at somebody who'd just found the golden egg when she wasn't even in the hunt? Maybe not. Did Elizabeth know I hadn't found it by myself? I hoped not.

I lowered the golden egg, and no longer smiling, dropped it in my basket. Then I saw Elizabeth turn, break her pose.

At the back of the room Papa was standing in the doorway. He'd come to let her out. I was glad.

One night that June I didn't go right to sleep. I heard Elizabeth quietly crawl out of bed. I peeped. She was wearing dark slacks and a blue blouse—not pajamas—and she glanced my way before she slid out the door. She didn't come back until nearly eleven, I could tell by the clock. Mother didn't catch her, and I never let on.

Four years later I was in Josephine's Room with Mother when we found out Elizabeth had run away, gotten married. Elizabeth wasn't quite eighteen. Mother sat at the sewing machine crying, her head in her hands. Then she raised her glasses, dabbed her eyes with a wet handkerchief, and said, "How could Elizabeth do this to me?"

"Oh Mother," I said, fighting tears. I sat on the trunk close to the machine, feeling like the bottom of my stomach had dropped out. Was Mother never going to speak to Elizabeth again?

"She thinks only of herself," Mother said.

"No," I ventured. My voice was a weak whisper. "Elizabeth loves you, even if she doesn't say so much."

"Selfish," Mother groaned, as if I'd said nothing.

I stared straight ahead at Aunt Bea's writing desk and didn't say more. I remembered Elizabeth the day of the egg hunt, how she looked in this very room, sitting alone in the front bay window, me outside holding up the golden egg as if I'd found a great prize, when in fact I'd only searched where Mother told me. And for one scary moment, I was glad of what Elizabeth did.

Ned's Kiss ⌒

A boy in our class, Grant Singleton, was going to have a prom party for his thirteenth birthday. Grant was the quiet type and probably didn't want a party at all, but his mother made big plans anyway. I even got an invitation through the mail, addressed "Miss Maggie Spencer." All week the girls at school discussed what they would wear. My friend Juliette bragged on her green-and-white striped dress. A few planned to wear long dresses, but Juliette and I didn't want to do that; the hems got dirty if you ran around the yard and the skirts could split when you jumped the curb. I hadn't yet decided what to wear. But I had another worry, something those in town never had to think about. They lived in walking distance. I was four miles away. How could I get to the Singletons'?

Early in the week I started in on Mother. "Who'll drive me to the party on Friday night? Will you?" I asked, trailing her across the back porch. Mother leaned over a box of spready maidenhair fern that was catching the April sunlight.

"Is it going to be well-chaperoned?" She picked off a dead frond. "Not one of those parties where you run wild and chase each other into the street?"

"Mother, this is Mrs. Singleton's!" Then I wondered what she'd think if she drove up in front of the house and saw a dozen boys horsing around in the yard.

"Maybe Elizabeth can drive me in," I said, hoping she'd go for that. Elizabeth was sixteen, barely. "Bird can ride in as far as Shing's."

"I'll have to think about it," said Mother. She started down the back steps. "And we don't know yet if Bird can go."

I took that for a yes, and grinned. Last February Elizabeth began driving into town on Saturday afternoons with Mother in the passenger seat of the blue Studebaker and me in the back. In March she drove in with only me. Then two weeks ago, Mother let Elizabeth drive to town on a Friday night with just me and Bird. Since Mother hadn't wanted to ride in herself, she'd asked Bird, our cook, to take her place. We didn't mind, and Bird liked going places.

We had dropped her off at her daughter's house at the edge of town; Shing lived on Wooden Lane, near the highway. Then Elizabeth skirted the corners with traffic lights and took me to Webster Street where my friends were playing kick-the-can under the street light. Elizabeth parked in the next block by Mary Louise's house, and they walked to the picture show. They met boys there, I knew, although Elizabeth never mentioned this to Mother. Elizabeth already had a boyfriend, Lewis; he rode a bike to our house sometimes since his family didn't own a car. Mother allowed Elizabeth to meet Lewis on Saturdays at the show, but she didn't know about the Friday nights.

Later that night, about ten o'clock, we drove to the edge of town, turned at the big tobacco warehouse, and picked up Bird on Wooden Lane. Climbing in, she called good-bye to Shing who stood in the doorway, embers glowing in the fireplace behind. Bird wore her puffy white work cap, as usual, but she had on a good dress with full sleeves that hid her shoulder growth—her goiter. Bird was supposed to be our protection, but she didn't know a thing about cars. If we'd broken down, she'd have just stood on the side of the road beside us, her in her bunched-up white hat. The sight of us might have scared some away. But the car ran fine, and we got home on time. Elizabeth and I had both said we'd like to ride in like that again.

∽

On the evening of Grant's party, we pulled out of the yard at 7:30, Elizabeth at the wheel, me beside her, and Bird sitting straight in the back seat, already staring out the window as though she was ready to see something new. I had on a dress fresh off Mother's machine— white, rosebuds on the collar, and a swishy full skirt—one I'd chosen over last year's blue, though blue was my favorite color. The sun was setting behind us and its yellow light streaked the dirt road ahead, making it look like a golden avenue to good times.

"Drive fast," I said to Elizabeth after we dropped Bird off. "This is going to be a great party."

"You better not tell Mother if they start those silly chases," said Elizabeth, hands firmly on the wheel.

"*You* better not let her know you're meeting Lewis," I countered. Then I added, "It's good that Bird rode in with us instead of Mother." Elizabeth nodded.

At the Singletons', seventh graders crowded the U-shaped porch and spilled into the azalea-edged yard. Elizabeth pulled up close to the curb. She smiled at how well she'd done that, and getting out, I grinned back. I was glad we'd already dropped Bird off. Somebody might have made a stupid remark, like "Who's that in the back? Has she just had a shampoo?" or sung-out, "Maggie brought her nurse maid, Maggie brought her nurse maid."

"Hey, Maggie!" Juliette screamed from the porch. She was standing by a rocker and waving as though she hadn't seen me in months.

Elizabeth groaned and drove off. She thought Juliette was a nut. Watching Elizabeth leave, I wondered what she'd be up to with *her* friends, who sometimes acted silly too.

"Come on," hollered Juliette. She looked pretty in her green-striped dress. She grinned, showing long white teeth, like a rabbit's, but straighter, prettier. Mother always said Juliette's mouth was too big and she hee-hawed. But I thought she had a great laugh.

I climbed the steps, my white skirt swinging. I looked forward to the promming, when in pairs we'd walk to the corner and back— maybe twice—then switch to a new prom partner. But sometimes a chase got started and we might miss a prom.

On the porch behind Juliette, Billie Faye and Jane were talking to Luther and Ben, both in Sunday suits. But the boy I noticed wore an open-at-the-neck blue shirt. The blue made his eyes look bluer. That was Jeff.

"Who're you gonna prom with first, Maggie? Jeff?" asked Juliette, too loud.

"Shut up," I said. The boys did the asking and I didn't want him to hear.

We walked to the side of the porch where Mrs. Singleton was passing out prom cards—pink on the edges and white in the middle with ten numbered lines, blank lines, waiting for names. Very blank. In a minute the boys would start asking girls for proms by number. I got the shivers, like before a test.

Jeff squeezed himself in between two boys in the swing and glanced my way when he took a card. Little goosebumps popped up on my arms—nice ones. He was going to ask. Still, Jeff was shy, and I didn't want Juliette scaring him off. To distract her I pointed at a boy on the banister wearing a tan suit. "There's Ned," I whispered. "He'll ask you, I bet. He likes you." Ned swiveled on the railing and grinned as though he'd heard. He had a chipped front tooth that gave him a reckless look.

"Oh, who gives a rip about ol' Ned," hooted Juliette. Suddenly she jumped to touch a Japanese lantern overhead. "See? I'm a good jumper. I'm going out for basketball next year." Smirking, she nodded toward Jeff's neighbor in the swing. "Melvin loves basketball." Broad-shouldered Melvin lifted one dark eyebrow, as though ready for more action than promming.

"Melvin wasn't looking until you *jumped*, but Ned was."

"Ned thinks he's hot stuff. I don't want to prom with him. He calls me motor-mouth to make me mad."

We talked to curly-haired Rose and baby-faced Gloria Jean until the boys, in a slow wave, surged toward us, prom cards in hand.

"Whee! I'm all full but for number three!" Juliette held up her pink-trimmed card, covered with scribbled names.

"Not so loud," I whispered. Girls usually guarded their cards unless they filled up fast, every blank.

"Who wants prom three?" she shouted. Juliette let out a hee-haw and skipped across the porch. "Anybody but Ned! Anybody but Ned!"

Everyone laughed. Balancing on the banister, Ned stretched his mouth with his thumbs and stuck out his tongue to make a face.

A shrimp named Edward ran up to Juliette, maybe to ask for prom three. The bell sounded, and I paraded down the steps with Jeff, feeling my white skirt swing. We prommed to the corner of the street, behind Billie Faye and Mack, and on the way back the four of us jumped the cracks in the sidewalk.

Number two, and I prommed with Richard, who played the clarinet. He wanted to hold my hand. I let him, but his fingers felt wet and cold. Behind us Wilda and Carl were bumping hips and giggling. Coming back, we heard someone playing the piano in the living room and through the window saw two girls dancing, acting silly, not minding that they didn't have prom partners. This was a good party. So far, no wild chases, which should please Mother. Still, I was a good runner and wouldn't have minded a dash around the yard.

"Prom three!" called Grant's mother, standing on the steps. She rang a brass bell. Mrs. Singleton was round as a melon and wore crepe dresses and rimless glasses, and was a favorite of my mother's because she went to our church. "You can have some punch after this prom," she called, not noticing that three boys already held cups. Grant was one of them; he hadn't prommed at all.

My prom was with Allen, a skinny school-crossing boy. He'd worn his patrol white crossbar, which looked pretty silly at a party. We started down the front steps.

"Yi-eeh!" someone screamed, loud and drawn-out, like a person who'd just seen Frankenstein. I froze. Another yell ricocheted. It came from the side of the porch where the punch bowl was, and the voice sounded familiar.

I turned as Juliette zipped across the porch bumping into people, her green-striped skirt flying out behind. She cut into the front hall. I glanced toward the punch bowl where some boys stood, laughing. One gave Ned a poke on the shoulder. Ned grinned and threw his fist up in the air like a winning prize fighter.

Forgetting Allen, I ran up the steps and into the hall. A white-bulbed chandelier shed light on an armchair by the living room door and onto Juliette's blond hair. She sat, head in her hands, already surrounded by three excited girls.

"Are you hurt?" I cried, elbowing through the girls.

Juliette's yelling had given way to a moan that somehow sounded more awful then the scream.

"Did someone hit you?" asked Wilda, pushing me aside.

Juliette made a choking, gurgling sound.

"Was it Ned?" I stepped in front again. "I saw him on the porch, swinging his fists."

"No, nobody hit me." Juliette kept her head down.

Gloria Jean, coming in from the side, touched Juliette's arm . "Did someone hurt your feelings?"

"Not exactly," she wailed. "Worse than that."

"Was it Melvin?" I knew it had to do with those boys at the punch bowl. "Did he say something bad?"

"Melvin didn't do anything!"

"Who then? Tell us!" Wilda stroked Juliette's hand.

Juliette raised her teary face. "It was Ned. He *kissed* me. I hate him!"

I stared, trying to take it in. I'd never been kissed except a peck on the cheek during Spin-the-Bottle, which wasn't anything. At times I'd given real kissing some thought—lips actually touching lips—but that seemed way out in the future. "Where'd he kiss you?" I wanted a clue. "On the lips?"

"Almost," Juliette groaned. She pointed to the exact corner of her mouth. "Here."

"That's not so bad," I said, hoping this was true.

"Mother told me not to let anybody do that. She's going to be mad! She'll whip me."

Behind us, Rose said in a loud whisper to someone at the door, "Ned kissed Juliette! She thinks her mother's going to kill her." Feet ran along the porch. "Ned kissed Juliette!" another girl called. A boy shouted back, "She threw some punch on him. That's why he did it."

Juliette didn't seem to hear. She sucked in a sob. "I better go tell Mother."

"Why *tell* her?" Wilda bent to look at Juliette.

"She'll find out. She always does. Mother said not to let it happen! She *meant* it."

"But you couldn't help it," I put in, "and it wasn't quite on the mouth." That seemed important somehow. But why was Juliette going to tell?

"If she hears about it from somebody else, it'll be worse." Juliette rose, touching the chair arms for support. "I'm going home."

"Wait," I said, and stumbled on the doormat hurrying out the front door. I wanted to tell Allen I wasn't promming. Juliette was my friend, no matter what. I remembered the time we ran out in the street and Gloria Jean was nearly hit by a car, and I told my mother. Still, that wasn't a stupid, not-quite-on-the-mouth kiss that might cause a whipping.

I found Allen lounging in the swing. Ned and Melvin were perched on the banister. "Ned kissed Juli-ette," taunted Melvin. "Now she's going to tell her mother. Better watch out, Ned!"

"Tell Juliette I'll kiss her again if she wants me to." Ned knocked his heels against the lower rail and grinned, so that his chipped tooth showed.

"Ned is Juliette's Romeo, Romeo and Juliette!" shouted a boy named Hugh. Somebody else picked it up, "Ned is Juliette's Ro-me-o!" People laughed.

"Oh, hush up!" I said. I ran back toward the front door where a procession was already leaving—Juliette, supported by Rose, Wilda, and Gloria Jean. "Don't listen to those boys," I said to Juliette.

"Ned's not Romeo. He's a dumb nut," Juliette spit out. Then she sniffed, wiping away tears, "You come with me too, Maggie."

"Can't you just stay here? You could call your mother," I said.

Wilda gave a big nod. "Or you could tell her later."

Juliette only wailed and said we didn't understand.

If telling was going to be so bad, I didn't know if I wanted to be in on it, but when they started down the steps, I swung in behind them.

Juliette's house was over a block away. Since prom three wasn't happening, the sidewalk was empty. Streetlights shone on the cracked concrete squares that led to the corner. We started out, one on each side of Juliette holding onto her arms. "Good luck, Juliette," Allen called from the porch, lifting a punch cup in salute, as though Juliette was entering a contest. "Romeo's Juliette," he added dumbly, and I gave him a glare.

We spread across the sidewalk, jostling to see who'd be next to Juliette; the end one had to walk on the grass. "Don't worry, we'll stand behind you," said Wilda as she edged Rose to the side. "Yeah," I seconded, getting in the swing of things. "Ned shouldn't have done that." Rose said from the grass, "Ned's awful!" In front of a brick house near the corner, Juliette slowed. She swayed, put her hand to her forehead. "Do you want to go back?" I asked. I thought of Jeff and the next prom.

"No-oo," Juliette groaned. "I've got to tell her."

"It wasn't your fault," I assured her, but in a way I was glad she was going home. Would her mother really whip her? I tried to picture Mrs. Alderman holding a big paddle, but I couldn't. Mrs. Alderman was plump and liked to tell funny stories on Juliette and Mr. Alderman. She laughed a lot. Could Juliette be mixed up?

We turned at the corner. Juliette stumbled on the buckling sidewalk. We hung on her arms and inched along. Ahead was a tan stucco house with a red-tiled roof—the Aldermans'. "You may not get a whipping," encouraged Gloria Jean. But her voice didn't sound like she believed it.

"You want us to go in with you?" I whispered, wrinkling my whole face. We passed the dark bushes edging the yard.

"You can wait on the porch." Juliette's breath was coming in nervous little gulps. Once, playing dodge ball, she got so excited she wet her pants. I hoped this didn't happen now.

We mounted the cement steps. A yellow light by the door shone on two porch rockers. "Do you think your mother will go to the Singletons' and fuss at Ned?" asked Wilda in a low, hopeful tone. Now that would be good, I thought.

"She might," said Juliette in her regular voice. Then she inhaled in jerky sobs. "But she'll get me first." We stopped by a rocker. Through the glass panes in the door, we could see Mr. Alderman in an armchair, reading a newspaper. Then Mrs. Alderman came from the kitchen in a frisky walk. She headed straight for the door. She must have heard us.

She swung the door open and her eyes widened. "Juliette, what happened?" She reached out. "Darling, are you hurt?"

Juliette stepped inside and ran her hand over her green-striped skirt as though this would help her speak. The four of us stayed on the porch. "Mother," she quavered, "Ned Terrell kissed me." She let out a moan.

"Ned what?"

"He kissed me, right here." Juliette touched the corner of her mouth. "I didn't know he was going to until he did. Honest."

We all nodded. Mrs. Alderman blinked. She scanned our faces, and looked back at Juliette. "Ned kissed you? That's all?"

"Yes, ma'm," volunteered Gloria Jean. "It wasn't her fault. He just did it. Well, she might have thrown a little punch."

"Are you going to whip her?" Rose asked in a weak voice.

Mrs. Alderman put her hands on her full hips. "Juliette, you left the party to come tell me Ned *kissed* you?"

"The party's almost stopped," put in Wilda.

"He didn't kiss her quite on the mouth," I said. I wanted her to know that.

"Juliette, you goose!" Mrs. Alderman rolled her eyes back in her head.

"Mother, you said *never* let a boy do that! You *said*."

Mrs. Alderman glanced sideways at Mr. Alderman who was peering over his paper. She gave a low laugh. "Juliette, I didn't say a boy couldn't give you a little kiss at a party. I was talking about . . . about something else." Laughing harder, she sat down in a straight chair at the dining table and leaned over. Mr. Alderman began chuckling. We stood at the door, looking at each other.

Juliette asked, "Aren't you going to the Singletons' and get on Ned? Some stupid boys called him Romeo."

Mrs. Alderman tried to stop laughing. "Honey, Ned's probably had enough of being Romeo. I bet he's sorry he ever came near you. You go back and tell him you're glad you were sweet enough to kiss."

"No-oo," we all groaned. I couldn't believe it. After all this, Ned's kiss meant nothing.

"Juliette," I said, "you sure got things wrong." I felt light-headed with relief, but I hated missing prom four with Jeff.

"Roll down the window so I won't hurt your ears," I said to Bird in the back seat. "I want you to hear how it sounded." We were on the way home and I was telling her and Elizabeth about Ned's kiss.

"Ei-eek!" I gave an imitation of Juliette's first ear-splitting yell. "That's what she sounded like, only louder. Then she *raced* across the porch knocking into people."

Elizabeth shook her head. "Juliette's crazy."

Bird laughed low. "Do that again, Maggie."

I opened my mouth wider and shrieked.

"That's enough!" said Elizabeth putting one hand to her ear. The other one had to stay on the steering wheel. She was laughing now too, but it was the way a grown-up laughed at kid stuff. Probably Lewis had kissed her before she got in the car to come home, and she hadn't screamed.

Elizabeth asked, "When she went back to the party, did Juliette tell Ned he was sweet to kiss her, like Mrs. Alderman said? Did she prom with him?"

"No, Mrs. Alderman didn't exactly mean for her to . . . just to act nice. But when we got there, Juliette was all jumpy and spilled punch on her dress." I rolled my window back up. "Nobody much was promming. Ned and Melvin horsed around in the yard. 'Ned,' I called to him, 'Juliette's not mad anymore!' But he just made a stupid face and kept on scuffling with Melvin. Grant was watching them. I think he was glad his party was about over. Mrs. Singleton was asking people to finish up the punch."

Elizabeth turned the Studebaker off the highway onto Spencer Road. We bumped once. Rolling from pavement to dirt, the tires made the gritty sound I associated with getting close to home. "I wonder if that was the first time Ned ever kissed a girl," Elizabeth said.

Bird chuckled and covered her mouth with the back of her hand. "I bet it be a long time 'fore he kiss one again."

"His kiss really broke up the party," agreed Elizabeth. "Next time he'll probably pick someone who doesn't yell."

"Not me!" I said, shaking my head. "Ned's a show-off." I wondered what I would have done if Jeff had kissed me.

"Are you going to tell Mother?" Elizabeth asked softly.

"About Ned kissing Juliette? I don't know." I doubted Mother would think it as funny as Mrs. Alderman. Mother had never even mentioned kissing to me, probably thought seventh-graders wouldn't dare kiss. She didn't even know about the Spin-the-Bottle pecks on the cheek.

"Getting on home now," said Bird.

I looked at the night sky in the direction of our house to see if there was an orange glow. I had caught Papa's habit. He watched for fires in the woods, fires that could spread to our house. In winter, driving home from night church, he'd look ahead at the dark sky and say, "Well, no fires tonight." Fire trucks wouldn't come from town to our house, four miles out, he once said. At times I pictured it burning, us standing in the yard in the yellow-orange light, watching the flames lick up the walls. Then there'd only be a pile of ashes, and we wouldn't have a home.

But the sky ahead was star-filled, no glow.

"Well, no fires tonight." Feeling safe, I said it the way Papa did.

"What?" Elizabeth turned.

At first I didn't answer. Then I said, "I guess I won't tell Mother about Ned's kiss." Elizabeth smiled. And, I thought, if Mother asked if we chased each other into the street, I could truthfully say no. One day she would guess there might be kissing going on, but not yet.

At Bird's house I stepped onto the road and folded back my seat so she could climb out. Our Studebaker was two-door. Bird leaned forward, bending her head, and her goiter swayed. I gave it a light tap, the same as when I was small. It was wiggly. "This still feels so soft," I said, glad of the familiar touch.

"Uh-hum." Smiling, Bird stepped to the ground. "You had a good time at the party, Maggie," she said, as though she wanted me to know everything was OK. "If you tell ya Mama, just don't holler as loud as that girl."

We waved and pulled out. Toward home the night sky looked good and dark. "Wanna hear it one more time?" I asked, cocking my head. I rolled down my window. Elizabeth groaned, but I let out Juliette's yell anyway, my voice getting higher and louder, and this time the sound traveled way out into the woods and echoed in the trees. I screamed until I almost couldn't stop.

War Prisoners ∾

On a bright June morning, Augusta Jones walked as fast as she could up Spencer Road, the empty pan she carried to work gripped in one wrinkled, yellow-brown hand. Sunlight bounced off the aluminum as she swung her arms. She'd left her own shady porch earlier than usual because she wanted to get to the Spencers' house before the truck rumbled up behind her—the truck with the enemy men. Twice this week it had passed her before turning off onto the dirt lane. Made her blood run cold. They were heading to Mr. Delmont's field. Used to be Mr. Frank Spencer's field. Mr. Frank oughtn't have sold that piece of land, Augusta thought.

She kept close to the ditch, her thin legs pumping under the folds of her skirt. In spite of the gray hair tucked up under her puffy white work cap, Augusta was spry. Sprightly, Mr. Frank had once called her, and her husband, now dead, had laughed his head off when she told him. "He mean you quick and mean," he had said. On either side, the woods this morning were thick with new growth. The lane the truck would take was still up a ways. It branched off to the right, and she could see where the ditch got shallow and the narrow ruts led into the hardwoods. No truck yet. When she passed the lane and reached the house, she would drink coffee in the kitchen with Bird Conaway, who would've finished cooking breakfast. She would put her empty pan alongside Conaway's pan, on the stove warmer, later to be filled with food, then start with the cleaning and the dairy work—popping in and out of the kitchen, hurrying the children out the way. Conaway was too easy on the children! Of course Gil wasn't a child she could pamper anymore, him being off in the Navy. Maggie was all over the house, in and out, but Elizabeth, she liked to stay in bed. In the summertime Miss Edith would let her miss breakfast as long as Conaway didn't fix her something later. Even though Augusta favored Elizabeth, she would yank the covers right off her. "Hump up! Get youself up!" Augusta would cry, "I gotta change the bed." Elizabeth would grab the spread tighter and they would fight.

From behind her came a noise—a rattling, a motor ka-ruping, getting louder. Augusta whipped around. They were coming, and she hadn't made it past the branch-off! The men would see her. They'd already seen her twice, and that was too much. Holding her pan high like a tambourine, Augusta scrambled down in the ditch, then up into the woods. The bushes grabbed at her skirt, brushed against her high-top tennis shoes. Those men weren't going to see her today. Wouldn't be grabbing her! She squatted behind a young oak, bending her knees deep, and tucked her head down so her white cap wouldn't draw attention.

The truck came bamb-a-lambing toward the turn-off, and Augusta peered through leaves. Plenty of men were in the back this morning, about a dozen—big hairy arms, healthy looking, like they had already cleaned up a big plate of grits and eggs. They were hanging onto the high side rails and jabbering; she could see their mouths move. Last time, the truck ran right up beside her before she knew it, and she heard one yell out something jumbled and foreign. It scared her. This morning all she could hear was the ka-wump of the tires as the truck bounced across the low ditch and took off through the trees. Augusta took her time, raising up. She pushed away a piece of blackberry bush that was sticking to her, then picked a single ripe, dark berry. In the road, the dust from the truck was settling on the ruts, drifting down in a pink-and-white cloud. Mr. Frank oughtn't to have sold the east field to somebody who worked enemy men. That was a shame. Augusta made her way out of the woods, eating the blackberry to calm herself down.

"They didn't get me 'cause I jumped the ditch," Augusta bragged to Elizabeth on the sleeping porch. Elizabeth had just crawled out of the bed after a short tug-of-war with the sheet. Now Augusta was smoothing the spread down. "Them yellow-headed men talking their funny talk."

"Prisoners of war, Augusta. That's what they are. Germans. They're not going to get you." Elizabeth, in seersucker pajamas, propped her chin on the chipped iron bed post and laughed. "What do they want with you?"

"They kill folks, don't they?" Augusta frowned. "They don't care if I'm colored or white. You watch out how you talk."

"I didn't mean that it mattered if you were colored or not. It's just that they're prisoners. They can't get anybody. A man is guarding them with a gun. They didn't get you those other times, did they?"

"You must think they'd jump for you, Miss Lady. Huh! They'd get me quicker than you." Augusta tossed the pillows to the head of the bed. "They'd get me while I'm by myself on the road."

"OK, if that's what you want to think," Elizabeth said, folding in her lips. "They're mean and they're after you!"

"Mr. Delmont, he's a mean man hisself. Now he's outdone hisself, bringing enemy mens down our road." Augusta yanked her broom up from the floor, ducked through the window-door, and marched toward the hall.

Elizabeth sat on the bed and took the metal rollers out of her brown hair, undoing the clasps and laying them in her lap. She tried to imagine foreigners, enemies, so close. The olive-drab truck had been trundling up and down their road for a week, but she'd glimpsed it only once, cutting into the lane, not near enough to see the prisoners. Augusta had really seen them! Elizabeth's supposed boyfriend Lewis, at seventeen, had managed to get into the Army Air Corps two months ago, and right now he was training to fly a plane to bomb people like those prisoners. And here they were, working in Mr. Delmont's tobacco field, doing whatever you do to tobacco plants in June. Several farmers had contracted with the government to hire them, Papa said, since they had a stockade full of prisoners out near Moody Field, where the Army was. But Papa hadn't hired any. He didn't grow tobacco, or much of anything since his stroke. Elizabeth didn't like to think of the stroke, how it had drawn the side of his mouth down. He could walk now, almost like he used to, but he didn't feel good.

Elizabeth picked up a roller and flew the metal cylinder through the air like a plane. She dipped it and zoomed it fast. Today, at this very moment, Lewis might be in a cockpit, learning to fly. She wished she could be sure he was her boyfriend.

The next day Elizabeth rode home from town in late afternoon, sitting beside her mother, who was driving the Studebaker, with Maggie in the back. Maggie was barely thirteen, a child. Elizabeth herself was sixteen, had a license now, and usually drove. But today, after picking her up in front of the Ritz, her mother had stayed at the wheel.

When they turned off the highway, Elizabeth saw a truck lumbering toward them, still a little way off. "Pull over please, Mother," said Elizabeth, sliding forward so that her brown hair touched the windshield. "That's the truck with the prisoners! Let it pass. I want to look."

"Where?" Maggie poked her head over the front seat.

"I can't stop right here," their mother complained, but she slowed and maneuvered to the side, out of the ruts. "There. But I don't see why you want to stare."

"Here it comes!" cried Maggie, bouncing toward the side window. "Germans, Germans."

"Hush," ordered Elizabeth. Maggie acted as though she were at a circus.

The square front of the army truck grew larger, and Elizabeth shifted sideways, putting a hand on the dashboard. It was going to pass close. She wasn't afraid, like Augusta; she wouldn't have jumped any ditch. Still, she was glad she was inside a car, not walking alone on the road.

The truck edged close to the ditch, one heavy tire in a worn deep rut and the other grinding down the loose dirt. As it gave the Studebaker a good berth, Elizabeth stared. A husky U.S. Army man was driving. He looked old, maybe forty, and a younger fellow with a speckled face was sitting next to him, holding a shotgun.

"Hey!" Maggie yelled as the truck rumbled by.

"Don't yell," said their mother, turning. She was wearing a black straw hat, and as she craned her neck, the wide brim shielded the window.

"Duck, Mother, so I can see," pleaded Elizabeth. But the truck chugged on. Out the back window, she glimpsed tanned arms on the rail, faded blue shirts, and some yellow-white hair.

"There *are* lots of blond Germans, like people say," Elizabeth mused aloud. Somehow she hadn't expected such obvious fair hair. Flaxen, that's what it was called. You couldn't really call American yellow hair flaxen.

"Dumb Germans! Go jump in a lake!" Maggie called.

"I told you to keep quiet," said their mother, wheeling the Studebaker back into the ruts. "Do you want to be punished?"

Maggie sighed and rolled her eyes toward Elizabeth, who chose to ignore her childish behavior. Elizabeth said to her mother, "Augusta acts like they're killers and we ought to be afraid. They didn't look so scary."

"Well, they *are* the enemy." Her mother's rimless glasses reflected the light with authority, and the gold nosepiece shone. "But they're guarded, like chain gangs."

"They're children of God too, aren't they? Aren't we supposed to be kind?" Elizabeth cut her eyes at her mother.

Her mother's stare lingered on the road. "I suppose so," she said finally.

ᴄᴡ

"I saw them close, near as you are to me." Grinning, Elizabeth stepped closer to Augusta, who was sweeping the sleeping porch, ten feet away. "I wasn't scared."

"You was in a car! You could get away. I'm just walking down the road by myself when the truck pass, where they can jump out and get me."

"Like this!" Elizabeth hopped over and grabbed Augusta's bony shoulders.

Augusta hit at her with the broom. "Stop! I'll whip you!"

Elizabeth backed off. "What time does the truck go back in the afternoon, do you think?"

"I be inside my own house then. Don't have to be on no road."

Elizabeth began walking the road about five in the afternoon. It was summer, no school. She wanted to get out of the house. It made her feel sad to see Papa, his hair fully gray now, sitting in his chair, resting his head in his hands. She didn't have much to do except write her presumed boyfriend Lewis, which her mother asked her not to do too often. Mother didn't want her to be serious with anybody. Lots of afternoons Elizabeth went to Benton's Pool to swim, and if she were lucky, to a baseball game at night with her friend Ailene, who flirted with the first baseman. Still, there was time for a stroll and she wanted to see the prisoners again. Even if they were the enemy, they were caught and helpless, and she might give them a wave, a tiny one, just to be kind. So many fair-haired men were loaded on that one truck.

The third day, she walked a little later than usual, and as she came to the crossroads, she heard the gusting motor behind her. Her skin prickled. She was on the road alone, like Augusta. This was like diving from the tower at Benton's Pool, although she knew that no crazed prisoner was going to leap down and grab her.

She moved close to the ditch to let the prisoners pass and glanced sideways. The men in the truck bed were tanned, talking to each other in an easy way, and a fellow with blond hair—yes, flaxen—stood in the corner nearest her, his arms stretched out in a **V** on both side rails. He looked healthy and sort of handsome in a foreign way, his hair shaggy and dipping down on his forehead, not how men in Georgia wore their hair. He didn't see her.

"Guess what?" she wrote to Lewis that night. "I saw the truck with the German prisoners today and I wondered what you'd think, training like you are to go over there and fight." Actually, she hadn't thought of Lewis at all when she was looking at the men.

Augusta clipped down one of the dirt ruts, was almost to the place where the trees grew thickest and the lane split them in two, when she heard an engine grinding, snorting. It was them! She broke into a run. Skirt slapping at her ankles, she made it past the turn-off. Panting, she twisted to look just as the truck bumped across the shallow ditch. In the back, two men were hanging onto the railing like monkeys, and one pointed at her and made a funny sound.

"You git!" hollered Augusta. Enemy prisoners weren't supposed to be sticking their fingers at her. She ran a few more steps. Then the men were swallowed up by tree branches.

On the sleeping porch, she puffed to Elizabeth, "Un-huh! They up to something bad. I was running beside the ditch to get ahead, and they point at me and make a WHOMP sound. I'm gonna ask Mr. Frank to shoot 'em if they do that again."

Elizabeth hee-hawed. "They were probably just laughing. I bet they don't see sights like that much—an old colored woman, beating it down the road, scared out of her wits."

"You mind how you talk. They after me more than you. You act like they ain't after me."

"OK. They're after you all the time. Why, I saw them yesterday, and they didn't pay me any attention at all."

"I told you." Augusta nodded, sweeping the bare boards.

"What time do they go by in the morning?"

"Time I leave the house, they must be leaving town," said Augusta with conviction. "They catch me on the road every time. Don't you mess up that bed I already made."

"Maybe around 7:30," Elizabeth murmured, sitting on the spread and drawing up her legs.

For the next few days, Elizabeth walked late in the afternoon. Twice she saw the truck as it flew pass, the same man holding down his corner, standing erect, his strong, sunburned arms on the rail and his yellow-white hair flying. He had a cleft in his chin. She couldn't tell if he saw her; if so, with her too-thin body and mousey brown hair, she probably looked to him like a little waif on the way to nowhere. In a letter to Lewis, she talked about the baseball games but she didn't mention the walks. Nor to her friend Aileen either, who went regularly to the USO dances. Elizabeth's mother wouldn't let her go, and because of Lewis, Elizabeth hadn't pushed it. Maybe she should. Lewis often said she was immature and too much under her mother's thumb.

On Saturday, the day Augusta didn't come to the house at all, Elizabeth rose early. If anyone asked she would say it was just too hot to sleep. She walked to the crossroads, a third of a mile away, and turned around. Sweat trickled down the insides of her arms as she got close to the lane turn-off. She wondered if they'd come. She'd heard they'd been weeding Mr. Delmont's tobacco plants and building a new barn. Maybe they took Saturdays off.

A second later she heard the rattle of the engine. Good, Mr. Delmont worked them on Saturdays! Elizabeth stopped, glad she'd worn her white peasant blouse with the ruffles. The snub-nosed olive truck drew even with her, slowing for the turn. She was in just the right spot. As it lurched across the ditch, she got a good look into the back, and the man—"Eric," she called him in her head—looked back. His eyes were as blue as the water at Blue Springs. Elizabeth felt flushed. If he'd grown up around here instead of over there, she told herself, he might have been a senior in high school when she was a freshman. He could have been on the football team, same as Lewis—so what was wrong with looking?

The truck churned down the lane and her view was blocked by oak limbs. Lewis's eyes weren't so beautiful, she thought, more of a liquid brown like the Withlachoochee River. But of course she loved him, although she hadn't told him so before he left. On their last date, he'd drawn himself up like a grown man and hinted that she may be too young to go with a serviceman who might never come back. She hadn't been able to think of anything mature to say.

In a letter, Lewis wrote, "When you see those prisoners ride by, holler out that they're scum. No, just get out the way. They're losers. In two months, I'll be bombing the hell out of Germany." He ended with, "Every night I dream about your soft skin."

Elizabeth locked the letter in her miniature cedar chest. She didn't want her mother to see it and ask questions about the prisoners or the skin.

The next afternoon, in white duck pants and a red and blue trimmed blouse, Elizabeth watched the truck approach, kicking up dust. What Lewis said came to her mind. As it passed, she didn't holler anything, and she held her ground instead of getting out of the way. But at least, standing there, she must have looked patriotic, dressed in red, white, and blue. Would Eric even notice, and what would he think? It was so confusing—that these men, the enemy, were now working in Mr. Delmont's tobacco field. Lewis used to work in some tobacco fields out another road.

Elizabeth thought of the saying, what you don't know won't hurt you. Well, Lewis wouldn't know.

Monday through Friday she walked at five, and at seven-thirty on Saturday morning. Eric held his same position in the bed of the truck, his eyes such deep blue.

Augusta marched along the road. In the distance, she heard the lugglug of that engine. The thing was rumbling up behind her. No, she wouldn't run; she'd run enough. She wouldn't jump the ditch either, squat down in the woods. "Save me, Jesus," Augusta said aloud, looking straight ahead. "Save me from these enemy devils." She said it three times, a spell against the devils, and they passed.

"They're not devils," said Elizabeth, good-naturedly, when Augusta told her. "But you're doing good, Augusta, not skedaddling into the woods."

"Skedaddle, nothing!" grunted Augusta.

Elizabeth laughed, glad she could talk to somebody about the prisoners, even though she wasn't telling all.

"They was a pile of mean ones in that truck," Augusta grumbled on. "If they'd a took it in their head to jump out, they might've run me down." She left with her broom, and Elizabeth dressed—culottes and a white shirt, tennis shoes good for walking, even though she wouldn't head up the road until late afternoon when Augusta was out of the way. Until then, she would read, sort through her *Modern Screen* magazines. She wouldn't risk going to Benton's Pool because she might not get back in time. Eric was watching for her now, she just knew it. He'd raised a finger on the railing when he spied her. Twice, he'd done it, she was sure. Somehow she didn't feel as flat-chested now, and wouldn't have, she was sure, even if she *wasn't* wearing a slightly padded bra. He made her feel like she was in a movie, a secret agent on a mission who fell in love with the man she was spying on. Like Barbara Stanwyck. Those other men in the truck must think it odd she was so often on the road, but she couldn't worry about that. Eric, so flaxenhaired, took her mind off Lewis being away and Papa sitting quietly in his chair.

Elizabeth tied her shoelaces, making a wish that Eric would notice her in a special way. She retied them three times during the day, making the same wish, for luck.

Late afternoon was hot, the road dusty. Perspiration on her face, Elizabeth stood on the ruffle of dirt edging the ditch and watched the truck roll by. Eric was in his exact same spot in the corner, an arm on each rail. They raised fingers. He did have a cleft in his chin, like Kirk Douglas, only nicer. Suddenly, something tiny spun away from the rail—from him? Elizabeth noted where it hit before a cloud of dust rose like a shield and the truck disappeared.

Quickly she pounced on whatever it was—a button, metal. It was dark and smooth and could have been from a uniform. She hugged it to her—her wish come true. Surely he had tossed it to her on purpose. Was it all he had to give?

At home she put the button into the miniature cedar chest, near but not touching Lewis's letters. If it came from a uniform, well, that was the uniform Lewis was gunning for. That made her feel queer.

"Dear Eric," she wrote later, propped against the foot of her bed on the sleeping porch, notebook on her knees. A lighted bulb dangled on a cord from the ceiling. Outside it was dark, the air filled with the smoothing hum of katydids. Elizabeth was glad Maggie had left for summer camp and the porch was quiet. "I call you Eric because that's a German name and I wish to call you something. You must know who I am. I'm called Eliz-a-beth." She pictured herself, in the movie in her head, enunciating carefully so he could understand. Did he speak English? Maybe someone could read him this note, if she could figure out how to deliver it to him. She might just wrap it around a rock and toss it into the truck. But suppose the guard arrested her. She'd thought about—almost seen it in her head—sneaking the car and following the truck to the stockade, then somehow slipping him the note. Or sliding it under the door. What door? She'd never be able to get the car! But Barbara Stanwyck would. She would talk to him through a wire fence, their fingertips touching.

Elizabeth couldn't think of what to say next. She closed the notebook; she would finish tomorrow. She supposed she should write Lewis, or her brother Gil at Great Lakes, but her eyes felt heavy now in a nice, contented way. Tomorrow she might walk early and late. Catch the truck both ways. Elizabeth said a quick, going-to-sleep prayer, asking protection for Lewis, health for her father, then thanking God that her mother was so busy with sewing and planting ferns these days that she hadn't noticed how often Elizabeth was on the road.

Augusta ran through the woods, lifting her knees high. Briars caught at her legs, but she didn't mind the scratches. She had to hurry. Panting, she came to the place where the road curved, not far from the house, and hopped back over the ditch into the road. In a minute she cut into the oak grove and slowed to a trot. This morning she'd skip right over her visit with Bird Conaway in the kitchen, and head for the sleeping porch.

"They're out!" she cried, jerking the sheet off Elizabeth. "The truck is broke down, right up the road, this side of the crossroads. The enemies all standing around, and the 'merican man sticking a gun to 'em."

Elizabeth's head shot up. "The man with the gun, he's not shooting anybody?" She jumped out of bed and reached for her shorts and shirt.

"No, but he keeping them in a line while the other man, he working on the truck. 'Bout ten of 'em standing. I was just minding my business, coming down the road, and when I saw what was ahead, I . . ."

"Augusta, hand me my shoes!" cried Elizabeth. "Don't tell Mother, please. I'll stay out of sight. I promise!"

Elizabeth hurried over the stile that Bird and Augusta climbed over each morning to get into the back yard. Running, she made it through the oak grove. At the curve, she slowed. Up ahead was the olive-green truck, but she couldn't yet see anybody beside it. She cut into the woods, running again, the way Augusta must have run, except she was heading the other way. The undergrowth was thick, and she shoved rough branches aside like they were toothpicks. She wished she'd worn long pants.

Staying in the trees, Elizabeth drew even with the big-tired truck. The hood was up and a man in a tan uniform was leaning over the engine, his broad back showing. She stepped softly. At the rear of the truck were the men, only six or seven, all in prisoner overalls standing along the ditch. The guard with the gun lounged beside them, but he wasn't pointing the gun at all. What a chance to see Eric! If only she'd brought her note. Elizabeth tiptoed to a perfect spot, hidden behind a tree—but not totally hidden if he looked hard—and she could see them all, not many yards away.

He was on the end beside a much taller man who was raising his arms, stretching. Eric wasn't so tall after all. In fact he was shorter than Lewis! Could he have been standing on a box or something in the truck? But he was handsome in his blue work clothes, his flaxen hair not blowing today. Really plastered down to his head. Elizabeth gripped the young oak trunk. She would stare hard and see if she could draw his eyes to her exact spot. In the movie, that's what would happen: Barbara Stanwyck would stare, and Kirk Douglas would feel the look and glance up, see her in the trees, though nobody else would, then act like he needed a stick for something and come into the thick trees while the guard trained his gun on him. Then he'd whisper to her, tell her where they'd meet.

Along the ditch the men moved from one spot to another, and one sat on the far incline. The guard wasn't paying much attention. Eric meandered to the center of the road, gazing up and down, but not into

the woods. Elizabeth doubled the power of her stare. Look! she tele-
graphed. She tilted her head, letting her left eye slide from behind the
tree trunk. She gently moved her hand up, then down.

Eric turned toward the woods, but he gazed blankly. That cleft in
his chin, could it be a bad pimple instead of a dent? Acne? Did German soldiers have acne? Elizabeth took a short side-step. Only thin
trees and bushes separated them. She slowly lifted her hand. He was
looking!

Elizabeth stood very still. Eric kept his stance in the road, his face
toward her. She had drawn his gaze! Suddenly, he snorted, bent his
elbows, and flapped his arms, as if he was a crazed chicken. How strange!
It didn't seem, well, polite at all. Elizabeth slipped back behind the
tree. She could still see through the leaves. Eric stopped his flapping
and stared in her direction with his finger raised, the same one he'd
lifted on the truck when he saw her on the road. Well, that was all
right, but now he was wiggling his thumb! What did that mean?

A roly-poly chipmunk-faced prisoner laughed, and another prisoner, a tall fellow with piles of dirty yellow hair, strolled toward Eric
and stared at her too. They must surely see the part of her she couldn't
quite get behind the thin trunk. The tall prisoner began wiggling *his*
thumb. And the guard wasn't even noticing. They could get away,
dash right into these woods, grab her!

Backing away from the tree, she heard the truck's engine choke out
a grinding purr. The army man banged down the hood and called,
"OK." Not paying attention, Eric and the tall prisoner took a step
toward the ditch, the ditch on *her* side of the road. The guard wasn't
in sight. They were looking, grinning.

Elizabeth ran. Two of them, then three, might be close behind,
chasing!

ᜰᜲ

The next day Elizabeth didn't take a walk. That evening, Friday, Maggie
got home from camp, sunburned and tired and hardly talking to anyone, except to say she had a good time. Elizabeth had actually been
glad to see her little sister.

On Saturday morning she couldn't decide whether she'd walk or not, and sat in the back porch swing thinking about it until Maggie slammed out of the screen door.

"You wrote in my notebook, Elizabeth?" Maggie held up a blue composition book.

"That's not your book, it's mine," said Elizabeth, but she recognized it and groaned. Jumping up, she reached for it. "Gimme." She didn't want Maggie to see the letter she'd begun, but she probably already had.

"No. It's got my name on it, if you'd only looked," Maggie said, holding it away from Elizabeth. "And for your information, Eric is a Viking name! Eric the Red, remember?"

Elizabeth lowered her hand. "It's not German?"

"Call him Heinrich or Ludwig. That's German, you dope."

"Heinrich. That sounds terrible." Elizabeth frowned. Had she really been calling him a Viking name? It sounded German. "I bet there are Germans named Eric!"

"See, here's my name." Maggie pointed to the cover, then opened the notebook. "Maybe I'll just tear this sheet out and give it to Mother." Maggie leered.

"Don't you dare, Maggie. You don't even know what it's about."

"I bet I do! I'll just send this to Lewis. I know his address. He's at Randolph Field. And you! Consorting with prisoners!"

"Maggie, hush. Consorting!" Was that what she was doing, watching them from the woods? Well, Augusta was consorting too. "Tell you what, I'll let you walk up the road with me next time, if you want to, or go to Benton's Pool with Ailene and me."

Elizabeth talked Maggie out of the paper, took it into the backyard, and tore it up. Instead of throwing the pieces away, she shoved them in her pocket.

An hour later Papa came home from town, after stopping at the post office where he'd happened to run into Mr. Delmont, he told Elizabeth. She had met him in the hall with a kiss. "Delmont says he's quitting with the prisoners," Papa said, talking out of the side of his mouth. He looked tired. "They finished the new tobacco barn, and there's not much to do until cropping. Anyway, the county is going up on the fee."

"The prisoners are through?" Elizabeth stepped backward, feeling awkward, unbalanced. Eric, or Heinrich, gone forever!

"That's right. They were having problems with the hauling too. The truck was breaking down." Papa sank into the hall chair, loosened his tie, then held out a letter. "Here, Elizabeth, I think this is from your friend."

Elizabeth found a quiet place to read. Lewis was coming home on leave! He was anxious to see her. This time she bet she would manage to date him every night he was here. She could handle her mother. And she would handle Lewis too. Still, she would miss Eric.

ᏍᏫ

On Monday Elizabeth got up early. She hiked up the road as far as the Bridge Pond and met Augusta, who was plenty surprised to see her.

"Eliza-beth, you outta bed?" Augusta bent over laughing as though this were a joke.

Elizabeth told her she didn't have to hop the ditch any more. No more trucks. No more enemy men.

"Je-sus!" Augusta said, throwing up the hand with her round pan. "For true?"

Elizabeth nodded. Then Augusta surprised her with a little disappointed frown. "Mr. Delmont soon be up to something else crazy, I reckon, but nothing quite like enemy men."

They walked to the house, Elizabeth holding Eric's button in her hand—not telling Augusta—and watching for the places in the road where she had stopped, staring like Barbara Stanwyck, when the truck passed, and mentally marking the spot where she'd hidden in the woods when Eric, or Heinrich, acted a little odd. Well, he was a prisoner, he had a good reason to act odd.

"'Bout here's where I jumped the ditch that first time," said Augusta, proudly.

Elizabeth nodded. Soon she'd be getting ready to see Lewis who was coming this weekend. Soon she'd be with him, and he'd see how much she had matured. Still, walking the road, she missed Eric—yes, that was his name, no matter what. She missed his tanned arms on the railing, the movie-screen flaxen hair, the clear, blue-eyed look he gave her from the bed of the rattling prisoner truck. She had stood right here, at this very spot, gazing up.

Lewis would never know.

Bird ∾

"Maggie, I hope we don't have to wait long," Bird whispered, leaning toward me from her chair. She held her white cap tightly in her hands. "I never even put up my mop."

"Relax. Mother'll do that. We've just got to get you tended to." I looked down at the coffee table to see if there was anything fit to read. General Eisenhower's round face beamed up from a *LIFE* magazine. A tear in the cover gave his smile a cocky, James Cagney twist. Why did magazines in doctors' offices look so battered, I wondered, picking up the *LIFE*. Over a year old too, not that this surprised me, not in here anyway. Dr. Turner still practiced over the corner drugstore, and this was the same high-ceilinged waiting room where I'd sat about eight years ago, a little girl with a swollen, hurting ankle. I didn't remember those faded blue curtains exactly, but I bet they were the same ones. The flowered sofa I was sitting on had a saggy dip that felt familiar too.

Flipping through the pages, I checked Bird out of the corner of my eye. She seemed to be studying the puffs of steam hissed by a crusty old radiator near the window. Probably she felt on display, a dark flower among lilies. She was the only Negro in the room. Three other patients—two old men and a big, hawk-faced woman with a bandaged

arm—waited in chairs along the opposite wall, but they weren't paying Bird much mind, only a look or two. I hoped she didn't feel too
bad. She hadn't wanted to come at all, said that the lick wasn't much.
While mopping, she'd slipped on a wet spot and hit her head on a
chair. The cut wasn't deep, but Mother talked her into seeing Dr.
Turner. Bird was close to seventy, thinner than she used to be, although you couldn't tell it from the waist down because her skirts
reached almost to her high-topped tennis shoes. But the bones in her
face seemed closer to the skin. She had bled just enough to scare
Mother, who asked her not to put her dust cap back on until she saw
the doctor.

I tossed the magazine back on the table and gave her a smile. "How's
your head now, Bird?"

Before she could answer, a pop-eyed nurse with frizzy hair stuck her
head around the inner door and motioned to the large woman. The
woman lumbered past us, holding her bandaged arm, not looking our
way.

"Maybe we'll be next," I said to Bird, even though the two men still
sat quietly, side-by-side, like old weather-beaten twins. Bird nodded.

The room was stuffy. The radiator clanged away. I crossed to a window and tried to open it. I tugged but it was stuck. "Damn," I muttered
and sat back down, propping my foot on the coffee table. Bird didn't
glance my way as I thought she would. She stared down at the dust
cap in her lap. That puffy white cap looked something like a shower
cap when she had it on, and she wore it all the time. I'd only seen her
hair a time or two. It gave me a strange feeling to see it now, knotted
black and gray twists close to her head with dried blood on one tuft.
The blood was nothing much, but without her cap she looked almost
naked, or like a fluffy-haired person who had suddenly gone bald. I
could tell she was anxious to get her cut fixed, put her cap on, and
clear out.

In a few minutes the large woman paraded back through the waiting room without the bandage on her arm, and the two men went in.
I turned to Bird. She looked scared to move, but not eager to stay in
that straight chair by the window either. "We're next for sure," I said,
"and don't worry. It's only Dr. Turner. Remember when he came to

our house once and got a cutting from Mother's rose bush? He had on a yellow straw hat and carried those big shears."

"I seen him from the window, but he don't know me."

"I bet he does. He knows all of us," I said. "He's doctored me too—strapped my ankle the time I fell off my bicycle. Remember?"

"Yes, I do." Nodding, she almost smiled. "I must remember better than you. We just told your mama you fell off yo' bicycle so she wouldn't know what you was *really* doing. Sliding off the roof of the old garage, trying to swing on a big vine, like Tarzan." She gave a low laugh, bringing the back of her hand up to her mouth to cover her bad teeth. It was as if this was our private joke.

I laughed too. "You're right. We must have told that tale about the bicycle so much, I began believing it myself."

"Your mama," she added proudly, "she don't put up with foolishness."

I stretched, then flexed my feet. "Anyway, Mother brought me right here to this office—I remember that part good. Dr. Turner talked a lot. Teased me about being clumsy and had me try to rub my stomach and pat my head at the same time. He could do it but I couldn't." I grinned. "Then he acted like he was going to strap my ankles together so I'd have to hop like a kangaroo. Sounds silly, telling it, but then I thought it was pretty funny."

Bird stopped smiling. "I hope he don't get silly with me. I just want to get out of here."

"Oh, I was just a kid and that was years ago. He's a nice man. Mother likes him."

The inner door opened, and the men shuffled past. Probably Dr. Turner had just given them some shots. I hoped he would be that quick with Bird. The frizzy-haired nurse signaled to Bird, and I helped her out of her chair. We followed the nurse down a dim hallway, Bird plodding along beside me, her head forward, cap in one hand.

A crystal bowl filled with white camellias sat on his heavy, lead-colored desk. Otherwise Dr. Turner's office looked pretty drab—but familiarly drab and comfortable, with the same kind of mission oak furniture we had in our house. The camellias on his desk were perfect, the dark green leaves setting off the petals' wavy whiteness. I figured he grew them in his own yard. His bushes would be tall and healthy, and he, like Mother, probably took cuttings, rooted them, and gave them to friends.

"Mag-gie, my dear, it's good to see you." Dr. Turner walked toward us with a huge mushy smile. He had watery eyes underneath bushy eyebrows. Before I could say anything, he was wringing my hand, then patting my shoulder and telling me in a wheezy voice that I had certainly grown. Except for the time he cut roses in our yard with Mother, I hadn't seen him since my other office visit. He must have said my name the same way then—"Mag-gie"—rolling out the syllables while he engulfed me. I suddenly felt like a clumsy kid again. His hair was whiter, his face more flushed, but otherwise he looked the same. Could he still pat his stomach and rub his head?

"How's your mother," he asked, "and who is this with you?" Turning, he grinned at Bird. No, I guess he didn't know her after all. Bird did a shuffling step I'd never seen before, like a dance step, or maybe it was a curtsey. She tried to smile.

"This is Bird—Bird Conaway. She's worked for us a long time." I told him what happened. "Her head bled a good bit and we wanted you to check her over to be sure she's OK."

"Well, Auntie, have a seat and I'll just take a look at your noggin. What were you doing, falling around like that? Maybe had a little nip, huh?" He chuckled, and motioned her to a chair.

"No, sir. Just doing my regular work, but I'm not as steady on my feet as I used to be." Clutching her white cap, Bird sank down in a straight chair by his desk. She straightened her long skirt of washed-out blue flowers and shot me a bewildered look.

"She does mighty well for her age, Dr. Turner," I said in a thin voice. Bird knew, and I did too, that although she didn't drink at our house, sometimes she had nips at her own house, then later waltzed unsteadily across our kitchen floor. Once or twice she'd fallen against the table, slopped the tea. But this wasn't one of those times. "She just slipped on a wet spot and went down," I said. "That's all."

Dr. Turner wasn't listening. Examining the cut, he asked me about Mother's flowers, and not waiting for an answer, described his new Queen Elizabeth rose bush, then began telling Bird in a silly high voice that he'd been doctoring cuts like hers for forty years. I wished he'd talk to her in a more normal tone. He was full of himself all right, even more than I remembered. "Why, Auntie," he said, "I'll have you fixed up in no time. Doesn't need any stitches—just a dab of medicine and a teeny-weeny bandage. But you better be careful about hitting the bourbon while you're hopping around the kitchen." He gave a throaty laugh. "Sure will tangle up your feet."

Bird shifted in her chair. I figured she was wondering what he knew. "Oh, Dr. Turner," I chimed in, "quit teasing. She'll think you're accusing her of drinking on the job. Bird, he carries on with everybody." The thought zipped through my mind that maybe *he* had been nipping some bourbon himself, but, no, I didn't think so. "I told her how you teased me when I sprained my ankle that time. You really made me laugh."

Bird's smile was faint. She pulled in her feet so you could only see the tips of her worn navy tennis shoes peeking out from under her skirt.

"Aunt Bird," Dr. Turner wheezed, "you know I'm just funning with you, don't you? I'm going to have you all fixed up before you can say scat."

Bird tucked her head and he swabbed on some dark medicine. For one second Dr. Turner was quiet. Then, lifting a roll of white gauze from a drawer and spinning off a long piece, he told us about being elected president of the Men's Garden Club, about winning a prize in a day lily show and how surprised his wife had been. Bird waited, head down. Poking under papers on his desk, he told a silly joke about clubwomen stealing plants at night. I wished he'd get on with it.

"All righty." Dr. Turner located the scissors and clipped the gauze. His eyes fell on the cap in Bird's lap and he put down the scissors. "Is that a hat, Auntie?" He picked up the puffy white cap and studied it. "You look like you might be going swimming," he said in a chirpy tone. "Is that what this is—an old-fashioned bathing cap? From the twenties, when they said boop-boop-be-do?" He let out a horsey laugh.

"No, sir. That's my hat I use for work. I'm going back to work when I finish here."

"Oh, now. Don't take life too seriously. You know—all work and no play!" Dr. Turner dropped the cap back in her lap, placed the gauze on the cut, and taped it. "Tell you what. Instead of that old cap, I'm going to put something on your head that'll make you look real pretty." He stuck on more adhesive tape. His toothy smile became broader, and he turned toward his desk. "Yes'um, pretty as a picture."

I had an awful thought. But no, he wouldn't do anything so crazy. The radiator behind me sputtered and clanked like some weird unknown animal in its death throes. I sat in silence. What confidence I had left was draining away, whirling downward, like a toilet flushing. Dr. Turner leaned over the cut-glass bowl and studied the camellias. Forever, it seemed.

Carefully he lifted the largest one. He shook off the water like a seasoned florist, and a droplet hit my nose. I didn't move. "Nothing like flowers to make a lady feel special," Dr. Turner said. "This'll be like a corsage worn on top." Humming, he stuck the waxy white bloom on Bird's bandage. One finger held the stem in place as he unrolled the adhesive. He taped it on. I sat mesmerized. Dr. Turner selected another, snipped the stem, and nestled the smaller flower beside the big one in Bird's knotted, gray hair.

Bird pulled her feet further up under the chair so I couldn't even see her toes and looked up at me in a confused, half-scared way. Her eyes asked me what to do.

I was a high school senior; I knew everything, I thought. But I melted into my chair, a sick smile on my face, and focused on Dr. Turner's hands—snipping, taping. He reached for another bloom. My gaze became stuck, and my mind wandered to strange things. I thought of flat gray tombstones with jars of plastic carnations on top, of a tacky corsage I once received, a decorated gardenia that looked terrible on my champagne lace dress. Before me, the crystal bowl was being emptied. Bird's head resembled a bouquet.

Scissors in hand, Dr. Turner stepped back to admire his work. "You can tell your mother, Maggie, that I'm not stingy with my flowers either. No sir. My goodness, Auntie, this is better than that old cap! You're pretty as a picture."

He was so carried away he didn't seem to notice Bird wasn't talking. Me either. I just wanted to get out of there, run to the car, and drive—keep driving on across the state line and into Florida. Part of me had already left.

Muttering goodbye, I floundered out of the office ahead of Bird and led her past the nurse, who whipped around to stare. We descended the narrow stairs, the plop of our steps on the worn rubber mat bouncing off the walls.

We started down the sidewalk. February air brushed against my hot cheeks like the cool breath of a passing angel, but one who didn't have time to stop and help out. Bird's head was tucked, causing the blooms to ride high. With my hand under her elbow, we progressed in slow syncopated steps, staring ahead, as though we had a walk-on part in a play and were making our way across the stage—a long-skirted, flower-topped colored woman led by a skiddy little person in green slacks. The winter afternoon was fading. A passing car turned on its light. I glanced sideways. She was the same Bird, but those camellias in the scrunched-up, crinkly hair made her look so . . . so different. That's all I could think.

"The car's not far," I mumbled. I wished she would say something.

We stopped on the corner and a station wagon rolled past. In the front seat a little boy pressed his nose against the window glass. As the car rounded the corner, I saw him grin, point at Bird, and say something to his mother. My cheeks felt even warmer; my jaw tightened. Bird's face didn't show any expression at all.

"Just another half block," I said and steered her across the street. Coming toward us on the sidewalk was an elderly couple, the man's hand at his wife's elbow the way I had mine on Bird's. They took us in, then stole a look at each other. The woman seemed about to laugh but the man rushed her by. Inhaling, I smelled her floral perfume. I knew it came from her. Camellias had no odor, only damn showy petals.

I gripped Bird's arm. We made quick time to our green Plymouth, parked parallel to the curb in front of a closed furniture store. In the store's lifeless window, I saw Bird's dark face reflected, the dazzling white top-knot, and a blur that was me. No one else was on the street. I swung open her door, then shot around to the driver's side.

Sliding in, I let out a sigh. Without thinking, I reached toward her. Without speaking, she bent her head so my fingers could get to the flowers, and I yanked the adhesive tape from the stems, relieved to be doing something at last. I could tell she was glad, too, though the tape stuck to her hair and must have hurt when I pulled it off.

Fingers shaking, I freed one camellia after another. As they fell to the car seat, I pitched the tape to the floor. "He's a fool, Bird. A stupid old fool!"

"Yes, I reckon he is." Head still ducked, she spoke in an even tone. I was glad to hear her voice.

"You can say that again!" The stem of the last flower slipped free. I scooped up the lot and slung them out the window as if they were poison.

Bird craned her neck and stared at the camellias scattered across the grainy cement; three were face-up, the white petals proudly showing. "Why'd you do that?" She turned her gaze to me, her pupils dark against the whites. "All them pretty flowers."

"I don't want anything that belongs to that old goat! Talking about nipping, then messing you up with his flowers."

"Now stop your fretting. He means well. He just don't *know* he's a fool—that's all." Bird picked up her dust cap from her lap, stretched it over her hair, and patted it into place. "Don't you mind."

"I couldn't help it," I said, fumbling in my purse. I didn't like the whiny sound of my voice. In the dim evening light, my indignation was fading fast. It had felt better to be just plain mad at Dr. Turner.

The car keys were at the bottom of my purse. I watched my hands go through the movements—fishing the keys out, selecting one, and sliding it into the ignition—as if my hands were someone else's hands. Back there, I had watched Dr. Turner's hands, busy with their work: snipping, tapping. And Bird, head tucked, peering up, her eyes seeking mine.

My fingers rested on the silver key in the ignition. The metal felt cool. Bird turned to look. "Just a minute," I said, dropping my hand from the key. A quick push of the door and I was out. The camellias lay forlornly on the sidewalk in front of the closed furniture store. My fingers scraped the rough cement as I scooped up all six. Two had brown creases streaking the petals where they'd hit the pavement, but the rest were still waxy white.

"You're right," I said, climbing back in. "I don't want 'em but they're too pretty to throw out." I shoved the flowers at Bird.

She rolled the stems between her palms, making a little bouquet. "Such nice big ones. Your mama will like to see these. She loves white camellias."

I felt a little prickle. Mother might want to know why I didn't ask Dr. Turner to please hand Bird the camellias instead of turning her head into a flower show. I could see Mother's knitted eyebrows. "How about telling her he just *gave* you those? How about that?" I asked.

"It's OK by me." Smiling, she leaned back in the seat, spread out her skirt, and relaxed. Her feet in the dark tennis shoes rested side-by-side, comfortable on the floorboard. Bird gave the flowers a twirl. "Pretty as a picture," she snorted. Then she laughed low, bringing the back of her hand up to cover her teeth.

She looked good, her old self and then some. My own face was still warm; from my cheeks to the tips of my ear lobes, a flush lingered.

It was first dark. I switched on the lights. Glad of the night, of Bird beside me—those flowers rendered harmless by her hands—I pulled out, and we rode slowly down the narrowing street that led to our road, to Bird's house, and then home.

Fardels ❧

Not many months before my cousin Gwen was in the fire, we went to the same summer camp. I didn't know Gwen would be going until the day I was packing to leave, when Mother walked into the bedroom with my bed sheets and announced it, quickly, precisely.

Gwen was deaf, and even on ordinary days all the relatives treated her special; now I'd be expected to do it at camp too. It wasn't fair.

"Noo-o," I groaned, grabbing the sheets labeled with my name and throwing them into my footlocker. I was about to say more but Mother headed me off.

"Now there's nothing wrong with Ethel choosing Camp Ochochee for Gwen," she said, standing over me. "You don't own it, you know."

"Aunt Ethel picked that camp *because* that's where I go." I tossed in a whistle on a plaited cord. I would be a counselor and swimming teacher. "Don't you see?"

"What if she did? It's a good camp. Plenty of children from here go there. Does it hurt to be kind to Gwen?"

"No." I gave her a put-upon look. "But Aunt Ethel didn't even ask me. She and Uncle Charlie could've sent Gwen to Camp Carlyle where they have real stables and sail boats. But no, they have to choose little ol' Camp Ochochee, *my* place." I slapped my laundry bag into the footlocker. "I'll have other campers to see about, not Gwen. It's not fair."

"Forget about fairness, for goodness sake. Gwen's friend is going, and she'll help her. I'm sure Ethel just thought it would be nice to have someone older around too, but you won't have to do a thing." Mother frowned, her mouth tight at the corners. "You disappoint me, Maggie."

My cheeks felt warm. "Oh, don't worry. I'll be good as gold. Look after the babies." I made a face but it was a funny face. I didn't really want to be mean, and anyway I would be at camp four wonderful weeks before Gwen arrived for the last two. Gwen's deafness didn't bother me as much as feeling saddled with someone young and green. Particularly at Camp Ochochee!

Camp Ochochee, a YMCA camp, was the usual—rustic cabins without plumbing in piney woods. A low mountain rose behind a squashy-bottomed, canoe-filled lake. It didn't matter that we ate endless beanie-weenies or slept on lumpy cots; Camp Ochochee was mixed—coed! Boys came from everywhere, from squirreled-away little places I'd never heard of—Dixie, Camilla, Enigma. Cute boys. Boys that, after camp, my friends and I would probably never see again!

I was seventeen, fresh from graduation, a big shot. My friend Juliette and I taught basketball, swimming, how to ride the camp's one old nag. Part of the fun was that you could flirt with everybody, and any boyfriends at camp were just part-time. If a fellow didn't work out, well, he might be gone on the next end-of-the-session bus.

Soon enough, the yellow bus brought the last group of campers up the winding road with Gwen and her friend Selena aboard, but no good-looking new boys. Aunt Ethel and Uncle Charlie would pick the girls up in two weeks. Gwen was barely fourteen—big-boned and blond, a little pudginess at her middle—but she didn't look bad. I gladly helped her get settled in her cabin, relieved that some of the other campers were paying her attention. They asked her where she was from, what she liked—impressed she could read lips. But after a day or two, they took off with their own friends.

"Ma-bie," she called to me in the packed dining hall. She couldn't quite say Maggie, my name. It was her fourth day there, and I was carrying a pitcher of iced tea past the table where she was sitting with the other new campers, including quiet Selena. Aunt Ethel was paying Selena's way so she could help Gwen understand. This past year—Gwen's first time in public school—they had both been timid freshman while I had been a wise senior.

"Meet at store, Ma-bie," Gwen said to me in her throaty, gulping voice. "I buy you popsick."

"Pop-sicle," I said, not too eager. "Right now?" I gingerly held the aluminum pitcher, silver beads sweating down its side. The evening meal—meatloaf for a change—was about over, and at my table the people were already leaving.

"Yea, I got mon." Gwen held up a coin purse—dark blue leather with white daisies on the side. Aunt Ethel really bought Gwen too many expensive things, I thought. I would have liked that purse myself.

"Well, OK, in about fifteen minutes," I said, but I wished she'd go off with Selena instead, shoot arrows or something. My friends were meeting by the lake before vespers. Later, way after taps, we'd slip out of our cabins, meet the boys, and make coffee over a campfire—the most wonderful coffee ever, made from a stash we'd sneaked out of the pantry, cooked in an old Maxwell House can. Gwen, of course, would then be in bed with no idea of what was going on. Thinking of sneaking out was so satisfying that I felt kinder to her. "Might make it in ten minutes," I sang out.

I left the dining hall with big-mouthed Juliette, and outside, we heard someone yell, "The T.B. girls!" It was James, the lifeguard, Juliette's semi-boyfriend. "Oh, shut up!" we laughed. My mother would have died if she'd heard. T.B. meant "tight britches." Juliette had on a snug white sharkskin pair, bought at Churchwell's. Mine were red corduroy, not as tight, made by my mother. We shoved James a little and told him how awful he looked in his frayed blue jeans. Then I walked to the store.

Gwen bought the popsicles—banana for me, strawberry for Selena, and grape for herself. Selena looked like a weasel, sucking hers, sitting cross-legged on the tiny porch, her long feet in high-top tennis shoes. She was the only girl at camp who wore high-tops.

Snaking out her tongue for the last drip of strawberry, Selena sauntered to the trash barrel to drop her stick in. Gwen balanced on the rail beside me, finishing her grape, and leaned close. "Selena nice girl," she whispered too loud, "but I get tire of just Selena."

"Shuss!" I put my finger to my banana-sticky lips. I didn't want her to offend her friend.

"I wish I had a boyfriend," Gwen said unexpectedly, glancing sideways, as though she *did* know about the midnight excursions. But probably she'd only seen Juliette and me horsing around with James outside the dining hall.

"You'll get one soon enough," I said off-handedly. I stood as Henry walked up. He was my boyfriend, sort of, and we would soon meet the others by the lake.

In the next days after swimming classes, Gwen surprised me by flirting some with olive-skinned James. He was nice to her. I watched from the far side of the H-shaped pier, where I taught a beginners' class. For someone with a little baby fat and not even any lipstick, Gwen looked pretty good in a bathing suit. Hers was a cute two-piece with tropical flowers. My mother wouldn't let me have a two-piece, not even the kind that covered a lot of stomach. My one-piece suit was new, though, and a nice shade of blue.

As I was finishing my class one day, I saw Gwen standing on the dock, her wet hair slicked back, tilting her head up to James on his lifeguard stand. She was doing her best talking, I could tell. He was smiling, showing white even teeth, but straining to understand. I was struck by how pretty she looked with the sun on her hair, the widow's peak showing plain—twisty little light hairs outlining the point. I'd always liked that widow's peak. It seemed so innocent, I couldn't say how. All at once I wanted to help her talk, even help her show off a little.

"Gwen," I called, walking along the wet planks. I took off my white bathing cap and shook out my hair. "You're doing so good with your swimming. I've been watching you. Show James how you can dive."

"Don't want to, Mab-ie," she said, frowning as though I had intruded. Her pale lashes fluttered. "*You* dive. James and me talk."

"OK," I said and dove in without even putting on my cap. I came up, spewing water, and Gwen laughed. She seemed to know I was being silly, getting out of her way. But, swimming off, I wasn't sure I wanted her flirting much, or I might look up from our midnight campfire one evening and see her on the opposite side, a coffee mug in her hand.

I didn't have to worry. Except at the dock, Gwen stuck with Selena, meeting me at the store sometimes to treat me. Once I bought her a Dixie Doodle. In August, when Aunt Ethel and Uncle Charlie drove up the steep gravel road to pick up Gwen and Selena, I stood by their Packard with my arm linked in Gwen's. Behind us, Selena was helping some boys lug their footlockers up the hill.

"Maggie, you looked after my little girl, I hope," Aunt Ethel said loudly, a fat arm propped in the window. She flipped open a Japanese fan and began swishing it.

"Ma-wa," groaned Gwen. "I no little girl." She yanked her arm free from mine as though she was angry with all of us. "I'm in high schoo."

"Ethel, Gwen's fine." Uncle Charlie craned across the seat toward his daughter, anchoring his tie, the way he did sometimes in church. But instead of church clothes, he had on a short-sleeved shirt. He smiled. "Aren't you, Gwen, young lady?"

"Yeah, I had a good time." Gwen relaxed and leaned against the car. "Ma-bie bought me a Dixie."

"Dixie Doodle," I nicely added, pleased Gwen remembered. It didn't hurt to stay in Aunt Ethel's good graces. Once she had taken me to St. Augustine when Gwen was at the special school there.

"Good, Maggie," shouted Aunt Ethel, slapping her fan closed. "Gwen, hurry Selena up. Charlie, start up the motor and let's get a breeze going."

Happily I watched them pull out, Uncle Charlie looking small as he maneuvered the car into a turn. I felt freer without Gwen around. Next year she might really be at a midnight campfire. Tonight I would drink coffee one more time under the bright, pineywoods stars.

At home I pasted my camp pictures into an album. One was of Gwen and me at the camp's tiny store, a dollhouse of dark creosoted wood. We were sitting on the steps. I looked like a true older sister, brushing Gwen's yellow hair from her forehead, gazing at her tenderly; but I suspected I was mostly posing for Aunt Ethel's benefit, in case she saw the snapshot. Gwen was looking straight ahead, one of her legs propped up on the other as if she were at ease, yet something in her posture seemed stiff. Did she know I wanted to be with my friends? I hoped not. I'd send a copy of the picture to Gwen and Aunt Ethel, I decided. Add to my good graces. After all, I had watched out for Gwen some and bought her that Dixie Doodle.

❧

During the fall, I saw Gwen only at church. We were in different schools, Gwen still in high school, and I, a lowly "town girl," at the local college. I was feeling small. Gwen, though, was filling out, stretching up, joining the band—of all things, crashing cymbals together. She said she could feel the vibrations. She'd soon be dating the trumpet player or somebody, I thought, half-smiling to myself, if Aunt Ethel let her.

The first of December Aunt Ethel telephoned our house and invited me to go to Atlanta. Uncle Charlie had already engaged my brother Gil to drive Gwen and her up on Friday. He was going to pay Gil. I hung up, glad I'd sent Aunt Ethel the camp picture. If I had used the sisterlike pose for a lure, I'd make up for it. I would be a great friend to Gwen on this trip. I'd only been to Atlanta once in my life! We would shop, stay at a fine downtown hotel, the Wineland, with two double beds in the room, and I could sleep with Gwen. Wouldn't have to pay a penny.

But Mother, at the sewing machine in our junky side room, shocked me by refusing permission. She pumped the treadle, stitching a green corduroy skirt for me. "We've just paid all your father's doctor bills," Mother said flatly, "and we can't afford it. No matter about the hotel itself, there'll be meals and all sorts of extra costs. I bet the picture shows up there are close to a dollar. I do not want Ethel paying for all that."

I knew money was scarce, but I couldn't shut up. "If Gil's going, I don't see why I can't."

"Gil's staying with Elizabeth, and he's driving, remember."

I groaned. My older sister Elizabeth and her husband lived in a tiny apartment out near Emory University. "Maybe I could squeeze in, too, and eat there."

"She doesn't have enough room for you both. Gil will be making ten dollars, not spending ten, which it would probably cost you." Gil had just been discharged from the Navy, and like most of the boys coming home, he needed money. Still, I was irked.

"I never get to do anything," I whined. "Gwen always gets to take trips. It's not fair."

"You're taking riding lessons, aren't you?" Pedaling, Mother glanced sideways through her rimless glasses.

"I knew you'd say that." In September, when I started college, I wheedled my way into taking a horseback riding class which cost eighteen dollars extra. I'd decided I could become a fine rider and had gotten down on the floor and implored, I was so anxious to find a new way to shine.

"What would you do in Atlanta anyway?"

"I could go Christmas shopping with Gwen," I said lamely. My money was in coins.

Mother snipped a piece of tangled thread. "Better do yours here at McCrory's. Anyway, what fun would you have with Aunt Ethel bossing you around?"

"I could take her bossiness for a couple of days," I kept on, but my mind was skipping ahead to the date I'd already made for the weekend; at least I wouldn't have to break it. Still, I hated missing Atlanta. "I bet Aunt Ethel buys Gwen an angora sweater," I grumbled.

"You'll have a new green skirt instead." I did like corduroy. Mother fed the ribbed material under the galloping needle.

As it came about, Aunt Ethel and Gwen didn't go shopping. Deep in the night, their first night, the Wineland Hotel caught fire. Flames swooped quickly upward. Over a hundred people died. Gil told us Saturday morning when he called.

At our house, no one ate noon dinner. Papa stayed in his room. I sat in the echoing hall while Mother paced—tap, tap, on the floor, then softer taps, on the rug. That Saturday afternoon my horseback riding class was scheduled for a trail ride, which meant we'd follow each other, walking the horses down a few dirt streets, into a park and back. I wasn't going until Mother, ashen-faced, said, "Go ahead. We can't do anything now. There's nothing to do." She sank down in a rocker. "I'm so thankful you're alive, Maggie. Please go on."

Later, I sat quietly on the trotting horse. I didn't tell anyone what Gil said to mother on the phone—how he'd heard about the fire on the radio, the announcer so excited he could hardly speak, and how Gil, when he heard the Wineland named, grabbed the radio and lost the station; how he and Elizabeth raced downtown, went to all the morgues where they were receiving so many bodies that ambulances were backed up in the drives; and how later he returned to the first morgue they'd visited. There Gwen was. She'd been in a back room before, being cleaned up. She'd been one of the first brought in. The firemen hadn't had to rush into the burned-up hotel and go searching for her through smoky halls, in blackened rooms. They did that for Aunt Ethel and found her still breathing. But Gwen, they just picked up from the pavement where she lay. The back of her head was crushed in.

A slender girl named Ernestine twisted in the saddle and looked back at me. "You OK?"

Her horse's name was "Two Bits," I suddenly remembered. "Yes. Two Bits is just faster than . . . my horse," I answered. I couldn't think of my horse's name. My brain was like ice, the channels frozen.

On either side, pine trees slid by. Switching the double reins to one hand, I ran my other hand along my thigh. I could hardly feel my knee. I couldn't feel the rocking of the horse beneath me or the rub of his flesh. "I have on my old brown jodhpurs and I'm sitting on a horse," I mumbled to myself. "Gwen is dead." I smelled the horse's sweat, touched the saddle, the coarse mane. If I hadn't spent eighteen dollars to ride this animal, I might be dead too—my skull cracked, my hair matted with blood, plastered against a marble slab. Had I bought my life by wanting to show off on a horse? That was hardly fair. But God hadn't asked me about fairness. What would it have been like in the darkness, in the air, hurling down?

At the stable I unsaddled the horse from the wrong side. He jerked sideways and stepped on my thin boot, not too hard. "Ou-ch," I yelled, grateful I could feel some pain. Hijinx! That was my horse's name. Or was it Jinx?

I'd never known anyone who *died* in their teens, died in the middle of a cold night. At fourteen, just before boyfriends.

ᴄᴡ

Late Sunday afternoon I sat beside Mother in the car in front of
Aunt Ethel's and Uncle Charlie's white two-storied house. Uncle
Charlie had hired a pilot, flown up with him, and brought Aunt
Ethel home. Gil was driving the Packard back. Aunt Ethel still
had some smoke in her lungs, but she was all right. She was inside,
in the living room.

Through the front window, we could see forms moving—Uncle
Charlie, one of the other aunts, maybe Aunt Mamie, even my own
thin Papa, one shoulder higher than the other. Our cook Bird was in
there, too, passing around something on a plate. They all seemed to
drift back and forth in a slow, mournful waltz, keeping time with their
steps, so no one stayed still too long.

"Maggie, I just can't go inside," said Mother, gripping the steering
wheel. Behind her glasses, her brown eyes looked flat as cobblestones.
Dark water over stone.

"Yes, you can," I said softly, feeling like a shadow. "You can do anything, Mother."

"What can I say to Ethel? Your father probably isn't talking at all.
What can I ever say to Ethel? My children are safe." She gazed at the
house. Then she got out and softly closed the door. "You wait here."

She didn't have to tell me to stay, I was so afraid. I wouldn't have
gone inside and faced Aunt Ethel for a hundred dollars. Seeing her
would be like being sucked into that burning hotel.

I watched Mother mount the brick steps. She had on a wide-
brimmed brown hat with a velvet band that she wore to church in
winter and sometimes just to go downtown. The hat gave her a
certain air, made her look tall and brave, like Eleanor Roosevelt.
Without knocking, she gently pushed open the door.

I stared through the windshield toward the west where, four miles
away, our house sat under wide oaks. Papa always worried that it would
burn and we'd have no place to live. But the house was still there, in
the December sunset, under a golden sky, and the fire had been somewhere else. A fireman had said Gwen probably fell from the fifteenth-
floor ledge. Before the fall had she stood there a moment, hugging the

wall, looking down into the night and the flames? Was it better that
she couldn't hear the fire trucks and the screaming?

Monday morning, Mother and I stopped by the funeral home, close
to downtown, on a block where most of the old places had been
torn down. Except for the black hearse under the porte-cochere, it
still looked like a fine old home with its fluted white columns and
wide front porch looking out on a lawn of dried-up winter grass.

Gil had been among the men who sat up all night. He had purple
circles under his dark eyes and now was slouched in an armchair in
the high-ceilinged hall. Beyond him, in the front room, the casket
sat on a pink-draped stand, two ladies from our church beside it,
talking quietly. Mother tiptoed to join them.

"Did you sit right beside Gwen all night?" I whispered to Gil.
For some reason I thought that's what he should have done. She
had liked his attention. Last year while he was in uniform, Gwen
had her picture taken with him after church, standing at his side
in low pumps, gripping a black purse by the strap. She'd stuck the
shot in her dresser mirror.

"Either me or Kenneth did," said Gil, turning his face toward the
front doors. "I sat on the porch for a while."

Gwen liked Kenneth too, his thin legs chasing us in all those games.
"That's fitting," I said. "She had some good boyfriends."

I breathed deep and walked to the stand. Mother was backing away,
but the ladies were still beside it, one shoveling a handkerchief into
her heavy purse. "Ain't she pretty?" she mumbled to me as though it
was her business to say this. "And to think, she'll never be a bride."

My face felt hot. I opened my mouth, working it aimlessly like a
goldfish in a bowl. Then I said again, as if I were striking a blow, "She
had some boyfriends though." How stupid to answer, I thought, as the
woman stepped away. Gwen didn't need my help now.

I couldn't look. Coughing, I hurried from the room.

That afternoon, at the service, the relatives sat in what had once
been a dining room, Mother, Gil, and I on the second row of straight

chairs. Bird and Aunt Ethel's cook were somewhere in the back, and Papa was at home, sick. In front of us, the first row was empty. An organ played "Rock of Ages." Then the side door opened and Uncle Charlie led Aunt Ethel in. The music changed, and a woman began to sing:

> What a Friend we have in Je-sus,
> All our sins and far-dels bear . . .

Aunt Ethel walked hunched over. She didn't even look as fat as before, but more pulled in. It wasn't cold enough for a coat, and she wore a gray dress without the fox fur that was so often draped around her shoulders at church. On her head was a gray hat, not a big hat like Mother's, but one with a narrow brim. She didn't even know she had on a hat, I could tell; it was as though someone had just stuck it on. I looked at her and knew the meaning of the word woe. She was woe. Woe was on every inch of her fleshy arms, her heavy shoulders. It was the color of her skin. She walked up to the casket, Uncle Charlie supporting her. She gave only one light sobbing cry. Where I sat, I felt afraid of her again, not because of her voice that bellowed at us if we didn't play right with Gwen, but because of woe.

She turned and came toward us to take her seat, and I scrunched down in mine. I didn't want her to see me. I was alive.

During the service I stared past the casket and out through a window that opened onto the front porch, where Gil had sat for a while last night. I pictured Gil and Kenneth with Gwen, her being in one of the rockers, them all rocking, and watching cars go by on Jefferson Street, people going into the Ritz picture show next door. I imagined them getting up after a while and going to a show themselves—the three of them, two boys and Gwen. It seemed real. What was playing at the Ritz? Once when Gwen was little, we went to a show, and a train came lickety-splitting toward us on the screen. "Ma-bie, watch out!" she yelled, ducking down in her seat as if it were about to hit us. Embarrassed me so that I slithered way down in mine, not because of the charging train, but to keep people from noticing me.

> What a friend we have in Je-sus,
> All our sins and far-dels bear.

The service was over and the woman was singing again in a peaceful, sad voice. What were fardels anyway? I didn't know. But in a searing second, I knew this song would always lay its mark on me, draw me close to the burning hotel. And I would see Aunt Ethel, weighted with woe, as heavy as Jesus's cross, staggering through the side door.

The rest of December, I tried not to think about what Aunt Ethel had told: how they'd waked deep in the night with smoke pouring through the transom, and when they looked out the window they saw flames popping out the floors way below, how afraid they were. They rushed to get wet towels and placed them around the door, but it hadn't helped much. Smoke pushed through the cracks. The fifteenth floor, where they were, had a ledge that wrapped around the building, part of a decoration of the old brick hotel, and they saw somebody creeping along it, hugging the wall, and thought there might be a way to escape. Large Aunt Ethel couldn't pull herself over the wire grating that was stretched over the bottom half of the window, and as the smoke became thicker, she told Gwen to go, please go, then collapsed over the radiator. That's all she remembered.

I knew Gwen had to make a terrible decision—to stay with her unconscious mother or go for help. She crawled out. Gwen's balance wasn't good. Probably she fell before she put both feet on the ledge. At least it was quick.

I couldn't think of it.

Winter quarter I took modern dance, not horseback riding. I didn't have the money for riding and wouldn't have taken it if I had. In a saddle I was dead weight.

Later, in the middle of spring quarter, we found out more about that December night. We learned it from a man called Red who'd been on the same floor in the hotel. Uncle Charlie hadn't wanted Red to talk to Aunt Ethel—not yet—so Red wrote a letter about what happened.

Gwen hadn't lost her balance on the ledge after all. Gwen, who had actually fallen off a log right in our back yard and broken a leg, had walked that narrow ledge, and walked it for more than a foot or two.

Red and seven others had gathered in a corner room. The fire was advancing, but the wind was sweeping the heaviest smoke the opposite way. Their room had been well sealed and they could still breathe the air.

Fire was popping out of windows as high as the seventh floor when Gwen came crawling in from the ledge. Red's wife figured out that she was deaf. She was having a hard time pronouncing her words, asking for help for her mother, two rooms down. "Is she a big woman?" Red asked.

Gwen read his lips and nodded.

"Well she's better off where she is," he said. Red kept everybody calm, and he talked out the window to someone in the room above, the top floor. If they all climbed up, they might be able to get to the roof and be rescued.

Using a sheet rope, and boosting and pushing each other, all nine, including Gwen, made it to the room above. People on the street said they looked like spiders scaling a wall.

But once inside, they found they couldn't make it to the roof because of the surging smoke. Red decided they had to go down again, this time down to a lower floor, and on down again to the firemen's ladders. It was a long shot.

They wet more sheets, made their rope longer, and tied it to the radiator between the windows. Gwen and the others had already walked an eight-inch ledge, then climbed a rope ladder to get into this room, and now they had to do more.

A woman who wore a black fur coat over her nightgown kicked off her shoes, said she would be first. "I'm going to make it, I'm going to make it," she said and gripped the knotted sheet. She lowered herself.

Red told his wife, Judy, to start down next, and to rest on each window ledge, and for the two women to alternate, one on the rope at a time.

When Judy came to the fifteenth floor, just below, she stopped on the ledge, and looking up, saw Gwen crawl out the window. People below began hollering, "No, no!" They had already seen ropes give way.

But Gwen started down. Through the smoke, Gwen's light hair shone, and her shape was visible. She grabbed the knotted sheet, tried to wrap her legs around it, but they swung free like two pendulums. Her hands slipped. Next thing, Judy felt Gwen's body brush her arm— a quick scrape like a lost, confused bird.

Red hollered. He couldn't see through the smoke, but he knew Gwen hit the pavement.

Distressed, he crawled down the sheet rope and helped the women back up. In the room, they hunkered down near the windows for air until firemen appeared on the roof of the next building shooting water in their direction. All of them lived. The firemen broke into Aunt Ethel's room too, found her slumped by the window, and carried her out, gulping for air. She didn't know Gwen lay on the street below.

I sat in the back porch swing, Red's sheets of paper fluttering in my lap. All that effort and then the fall. Was it better that Gwen did what she did, and then died anyway? That didn't seem right. If I'd been there, would it have been different?

The following summer I went to Camp Ochochee again. I was eighteen. I had a pretty good time, but I stayed away from the stable. We still slipped out at night, made coffee in cans over campfires, and it tasted OK.

The last night of camp I didn't get up at twelve to meet James and the others. I lay on my cot staring at the cabin ceiling, at the one sliver of moonlight in the air that seemed to be uselessly inviting me outside. I didn't move. In the beds along the far wall, my campers were asleep, breathing deeply, but I couldn't see them. In a moment the moonlight faded and all around was the night, the dark. But it was a warm darkness with katydids making their soothing, chirpy noises— not a cold December night, like the one Gwen suffered, the only heat the fire, galloping up the stairs, smoking the rooms, baking the walls.

I saw Gwen on the ledge, trying not to look down. Side-step by side-step, hanging on. Fingers digging into the wall's stucco trim. Flames sprouting like hungry red tongues out of the windows below. I could see them lick up the sides of the old brick hotel, and see her white face, corn-colored hair blowing back from her little widow's peak. She probably had on her flannel pajamas, didn't even know she was cold.

Was she barefoot? I could feel my own bare feet. They were on the ledge too, touching the grit. My legs shook at the thought. Even my toes trembled. I could hear the noise that she couldn't—yells from below, the screaming, the sirens. Then I was behind her in the smoky top floor room. Red was dropping the sheet rope out the window, the two women starting down. Gwen was crawling out on the window sill. "Don't go!" I cried from behind, but she couldn't hear me. I wasn't where she could read my lips. Why hadn't we ever taught her how to go down a rope? She was grabbing hold of the knotted sheet. I reached for her. She was gone.

And I was in my cot, staring again at the dark ceiling.

When I returned home, I pasted camp pictures in my photo book and showed them to Elizabeth, who was visiting. We were sitting in the back porch swing. Elizabeth was "expecting," her stomach like a small melon under her maternity smock. That was Mother's word, "expecting."

"Here's the lifeguard, James, the one Gwen liked," I said, pointing. James stood with a hand propped against his stand, a boat paddle in the other hand, and three of us crowded around him, all grinning and acting like we wanted the paddle.

"Did you tell him?"

"Yes. He knew some of the story. I told him how much Gwen did before she fell, and how she almost made it."

Abruptly I turned back to last year's picture, the one with me sitting on the store steps, brushing back Gwen's hair. "There she is," I said softly. Elizabeth and I looked at the picture a long time.

"Do you remember how we used to get mad at her when she was little?" asked Elizabeth. "She would get her way and give us that smirky grin."

"Yeah," I said, relieved to be finding some fault. It made Gwen real. "When Aunt Ethel bossed us around, she enjoyed it."

"Not always. She was growing out of it," said Elizabeth in a motherly tone.

I nodded, feeling grieved again. Gwen would now be frozen in my mind. No more progress, never older than fourteen.

"We should have taught her to climb better." Elizabeth pushed against the straw rug with her feet, swinging us, and rubbed her eyes with the back of her hands.

"For someone who couldn't climb so good, she did wonderful," I said. Then I almost smiled. "Do you think she can hear me say that?"

"She can't hear, remember? And she wouldn't like you to imply she was clumsy."

I closed the album, emptying my eyes of the painful and good picture—Gwen and me on the steps of the store.

I told Elizabeth how I'd changed my seat in church to keep from sitting behind Aunt Ethel. When the weather was cool, she didn't wear her fox fur anymore. Her shoulders looked bare, and I kept imagining those same shoulders in a nightgown, slumped over the radiator in that room, and Gwen having to decide what to do. Then she crawled out. If Gwen had fallen right off, it would have seemed like fate, a strike of lightning, but she did so much and than fell anyway.

"It doesn't seem fair," Elizabeth said softly, before I could say it.

"No! Nothing is. Gwen was put through a lot for nothing. God isn't fair." I pushed angrily with my feet, and we swung high. "But then," I said, "if He were fair, I might be dead too, instead of being alive because I paid money to ride a stupid horse." I began to cry. "Now I can't get near one, not that it matters."

Elizabeth pulled my head down in her lap. She didn't know much about fairness, she said, but she did know it was all right for me to be alive. Elizabeth rubbed my spine, all the way down and back up again until my skin began to tingle. Mother used to do that sometimes when I was sick and aching. It felt good. "You'll be a pretty good mama, Elizabeth," I mumbled.

I turned my head in her lap enough to talk and began telling her about Red's letter—a paragraph he had tacked on at the end. After Gwen had fallen, and Red and the others were up in the top floor room, waiting, feeling awful, there came a time when he completely gave up hope. The fire was coming. They would die too, he thought. He decided to do something. He pulled his wallet from his pocket and took out the bills—five hard-earned twenties that he had planned to spend on this trip. Walking to a window, he balled up the first bill, then dropped it out, hoping it would land at someone's feet on the cold sidewalk below. He went to each window and dropped out another; he did it four more times. "I felt like somebody down there should have a good day," he said in the letter.

We were swinging lightly, Elizabeth barely pushing against the mat. "I feel like he dropped one to me," she said. "That makes me feel good—what he did, when he felt hopeless."

"Me, too, just a little," I said, sitting up.

Years later, I noticed there had been a slight change in the words to the hymn, "What a Friend We Have in Jesus." The second line didn't use the word "fardels" anymore; too old-fashioned, I guessed. They'd replaced it with griefs. The line said, "All our sins and griefs to bear."

I'd never known what a fardel was anyway, but I'd had a sense of it. It sounded heavy, and I pictured a character in a Thomas Hardy novel lugging a loaded sack through a bleak countryside. I looked up fardel in the dictionary. Burden, it said. I didn't have a whole sack of them myself, but one was there, way down in the burlap.

I never heard anyone comment on the change of words. In church the people just sang along as if the line had always been that way. I said nothing about it aloud, but whenever we sang that hymn, under my breath I sang it "fardels."

Tiger Lilies ∾

One spring, a year or so before we moved to town, Mother planted tiger lilies. She left the front yard to camellias—the new rootings shielded by up-turned, blue glass battery jars; the back porch she left to her geraniums and wispy maidenhair fern, and planted the lily bulbs in the garden, close to the larkspur. They came up quickly—vivid orange, overpowering the lavender larkspur, not at all sweet and demure like the Easter lilies I'd thought they would resemble. The stalks were tall and thick, the blooms wide open with long brown stamens shooting up from the brilliant speckled throats. I was surprised Mother liked them. Even the name—tiger lily—seemed florid, the opposite of prim maidenhair fern. She loved the way they bloomed, no matter what, she said; camellias had to be coaxed along. In April the lilies grew in abundance, several flowers on one stalk, and she would cut bunches for the table.

The next spring we started talking about selling our place. Six years before, Papa and his brothers had divided the land. Then we made some piecemeal sales and kept only a few hundred acres, partly woods—not enough to make any money farming with our old equipment. The house needed repairs. None of the uncles wanted to buy the remains of Spencerwood, although each suggested one of the others should. I was twenty-one, finishing college in town, Elizabeth was in Atlanta, and Papa was gone, leaving behind empty fields and the soft scent of talcum in the bed where he died. That left Gil, Mother, and me.

Usually Mother was outspoken, too much. But when we talked at the dinner table about selling, she would glance away and make an offhand comment, often in a huffy tone—about a loud boy in her Sunday School class, or how Bird had made the biscuits too thick—and then walk to the back porch and water ferns. She seemed detached, backing off, but with a prickliness underneath. Maybe she would just rather fool with her flowers than get involved in moving. Still, I worried. Mother was in her early sixties, a time of life, I'd read, when it would be easy to slip into a foggy old age.

The Saturday when the talking got serious, Mother had picked some peachy-orange tiger lilies for the dining table. They weren't arranged, just plopped in a chipped blue vase, which for them looked right. We had listed the house and land with a real estate agent a month before, then pushed it out of our minds. No one would make an offer soon. But at the dinner table on that sunny April noon, Gil said a man from out-of-town had actually made a bid, named a price that was only slightly lower than ours.

Suddenly, my brother was out of his chair, pacing toward the pot-bellied stove that heated the dining room when it was cold. He looked eighteen, not twenty-eight, and worried. Gil pushed back his dark hair and put on his best man-of-the house voice. "We'll just keep it. I'll get more help with the farming."

"Yeah, we'll keep it," I echoed, caught up in the moment, although I knew most of our plows and harrows were rusting under the carriage shelter.

Gil's face brightened. "We'll manage somehow. Maybe we can buy a small tractor," he said and slid open the pocket door to the living room as though eager to escape. Probably he didn't want us to ask how we'd pay for the tractor.

After Gil left, Mother leaned toward me from her chair. "Did you see him smile?" She smiled herself. For a moment her face—

thinner since Papa died—looked soft and alert. "He's glad we're not moving yet."

"How about you, Mother? Are you glad?"

"Huh! I just try to live like the Bible says—don't give any thought to where you lay your head." She rose. An orange bloom fell from the vase and she reached to stick the green stem back in. "I'm going out to pick more of these."

In November, the camellias bloomed—pure white ones, lovely and cool as alabaster. Japonicas, Mother called them. She floated three in water in a low glass bowl and set them on the table. It was a chilly Friday, the day after Thanksgiving, and Bird had built a fire in the pot-bellied stove in the dining room.

Gilbert, off the phone, walked in solemnly and sat down at his place. "That was the real estate agent," he said. "They accepted our price."

"But was that our best price?" I said in a high voice, the part of me wanting to stay taking over. Another part wanted to live in town close to my friends. "Was it?" I turned from Gil to Mother, seated at the other side of the table. Gil had taken Papa's place at the head, and nobody sat in Elizabeth's spot. Mother stared ahead.

"They'll pay what the agent has listed." Gilbert rubbed two fingers up and down his forehead the way Papa used to. "We could refuse, I guess." Gil's big brown eyes searched Mother's face, then mine.

Those old plows weren't enough, I knew, and inside, I thought Gil knew it too. But I hated to see his face go slack. "Isn't it too late to back out?" I asked softly.

Gil inclined his head an inch. He didn't answer.

"Who is it?" I asked.

"A group. They're going to use this as a hunting club." He raised his upper lip when he said club. I figured he was saying good-bye to his own hunting in our woods—good, forested hammock land, Papa used to proudly say.

"Mother?" I hoped she'd say something instead of retreating to her flowers. This was too big a step for just Gil and me.

"Mother what?" She gave an abrupt shrug. "I'm going to plant some ferns in pots." Rising, Mother touched her hair—the gray-brown braids, always crossed in the back, then brought to the front and pinned.

I turned to Gil "Do you think she means to take the pots with her when we move?" That was stupid, but my mind was addled, my eyes filling with tears.

Gil shook his head. It was as if he couldn't think about another thing.

In January we made lists of furnishings to sell. Mostly Gil and I did. Mother acted like a guest in the house, as though she'd been one during all the years she'd lived here—through all the helping with homework and sewing in Josephine's Room and driving into town and fussing with Papa and reading in the back porch swing and bossing Bird around—as though this place had always belonged to the Spencers, not her. She bothered me and made me kind of mad. All she'd done so far was to stick some camellia cuttings in blue-glass battery jars and nurse them along. Finally she did say she wanted to keep her Singer. I wasn't sure there would be room in our new house in town, but I kept my mouth shut. The house wouldn't be finished for three months, and during that time, while we lived in a furnished place, all the pieces we were keeping would be stored in the smokehouse. The buyers had agreed to let us use it. Furniture would be carried to the smokehouse and covered with old sheets. The sewing machine was just one more thing.

Moving day, in late February, came drizzly and almost warm. Everything was a mess. I didn't have time to think about how I felt—probably a good thing. I might have cried. Gil had to leave at nine o'clock because a special sale was going on at Western Auto where he worked. "You'll have to do it, Maggie," he said. "They can't start yet, but as soon as the drizzle lets up, Mitch and Ezra will load the wagon. Don't let them move stuff in the rain. And you know what pieces are being sold." Gil shook his head. "Mother's just not paying any attention."

Gil drove off, and I went to the back porch to check the weather. Mother was watering ferns, and she smiled—a good sign, I thought. But she over-watered and kept poking at the soil as though she didn't want to miss this last chance to tend her favorites. Bending over the green fronds, Mother first asked about the chickens, a sudden concern, then jumped into questioning me about our old windmill. How tall was it anyway, she wanted to know. She scared me a little. "I don't know how tall it is, Mother," I said, impatient even in my fear. "I sure don't have time to find out today." She lifted her chin and marched toward Josephine's Room.

It stopped raining at ten. Wagons pulled up to the front and back steps at the same time. I hurried to find Mother and stopped at the door of Josephine's Room. Sitting at her machine, she was sorting through spools of bright thread. She lifted a strand to the milky February light to check the color, then she placed the spool in a little gold cardboard box as if she were packing it. Peering through her glasses— slipped down on her nose—she looked old and intent. But she wasn't intent on much else besides thread. I shouted, "Can you help? The Donaldsons are coming for your bedroom suite."

Taking her time, she wound navy thread around a silver bobbin. "Help how?" she said, as though I was making an odd request. "Can't you get Bird or Augusta?" She eyed me through her rimless glasses.

Suddenly I wanted to sit on the floor beside her. The nose piece of those glasses had formed little dips on the sides of her nose. I knew the places. I used to massage them with my finger to see if the skin would smooth out. It wouldn't. I lowered my voice. "They're busy. I only wanted you to stand at the door while the Donaldsons load their wagon. Be sure they take the bed, the chest of drawers, and the vanity, and no more."

Mother picked up a bobbin wound with red thread. "Maggie, don't forget this machine will be going into town."

"It'll go in the smokehouse first," I said, keeping my voice even. "Please, please, come watch the Donaldsons load."

She put down the bobbin and gave me a business-like stare. "Have they paid?"

"No." I was glad she'd asked. "Why don't you collect the money?"

"It's eighty-five dollars, I believe." She replaced the lid on the gold box of thread and stood.

She'd gotten the amount right! And no more talk about chickens or windmills.

Rushing down the hall, I almost fell over Augusta, who was on her hands and knees rolling up a worn, diamond-patterned rug. "Mind out!" she said, throwing up a withered hand. Augusta cleaned for us and worked in the dairy room, straining milk and making clabber. She was small and feisty and her high cheekbones gave her a hawklike Indian look. I paused, mid-hall. You didn't mess with Augusta. "I'm taking this rug to the kitchen," she said, rolling it. "Conaway bought it." Conaway was Bird's name. They called each other by their last names in a cheerful way, as though this put them in a special league.

"Can I pass now?" My voice rose. "I have to hurry."

"You better slow down, take it easy. Your Mama, she just water her flowers." Augusta gave the rug a last flip.

"That's why I have to run."

Augusta shouldered the rug and started for the kitchen, one rolled end hanging down her back like a long, fat sausage. I raced past her to the back porch. Mitch and his gristly friend Ezra were carrying the hall tree down the steps, one at each end, their muscles bunched and brown. Grunting, they heaved it onto the wagon bed, next to a sideboard. Those large pieces didn't sit steady. Luckily this trip was only across the yard to the smokehouse. Standing on the steps, I held out my hand to check for raindrops—none, so I motioned them to start.

Mother stationed herself by the front door. The Donaldsons' wagon, the driver's seat an old kitchen chair, sat at the steps, and their two teen-aged sons, Peter and Paul, were steering the mahogany veneer bed into the upper hallway. I watched from the back door. I knew exactly where the veneer was peeling—along a crack on the headboard. When I was small, I would run my finger along the crack and tear off a piece myself until Mother made me stop. That was mostly during the night when I couldn't sleep, and I slid in beside Mother. Good-bye bed, I mouthed. Strange, to think the Donaldsons would soon be sleeping in it. The little son, Troke, passed Mother, carrying the slats. She nodded as if she were counting pieces, not saying good-bye to the bed.

Would Mother get used to living in town? There would be no long boxes of wispy maidenhair fern on an endless back porch, no wealth of camellias, no fierce tiger lilies. For that matter, how would I like it? Half of me wanted to go, but the other half clung to the fence by the stile—the stile Bird always climbed to come into our yard. "I've bumped up that road one more time," Bird would say—used to say.

The rain was holding off. Under gray skies, Mitch's wagon, carrying the hall tree, churned across the dirt yard to the smokehouse. Papa's walnut bed and dresser sat near the back steps, waiting. I breathed deep. We were getting along without Gil. At the front porch the Donaldsons pulled off. "Git, now," called Ed Donaldson, sitting in the kitchen chair, slapping the reins. The brown mule lurched, wheels groaned, and the two boys standing in the back steadied the vanity. I watched them rock across the front yard heading toward a lane between pines. The wagon became smaller, the bureau and the vanity still seeming tall.

Mother and I walked down the shadowy hall. The last rug had disappeared and our footsteps echoed.

"You have the eighty-five dollars?" I asked.

"Yes, they paid." Then she raised both hands to her cheeks. "Oh, my goodness. I put the money in the vanity drawer!"

I ran to the front door. Beyond the clearing, no wagon was in sight. Mother would be upset if we lost eighty-five dollars. At least I thought she would, but she might simply go back to neatly packing spools of thread.

"I'll stop them," I cried. "Go to the back porch and watch Mitch and Ezra. *Watch* them! Papa's stuff is next, but if it starts raining, don't let them load."

I raced to the front yard where Gil's jeep sat—World War II surplus—the keys in it. I caught up with the Donaldsons on the first curve.

When I returned, Mother was on the back porch picking dead leaves off geraniums. Beyond her, raindrops streaked the lead-colored sky. "I caught 'em just in time," I said, slamming the screen door. "I have it."

"Have what?" She broke off a brown leaf.

"This," I said, holding out the wad of green bills. The sound of wheels crunching dirt came from behind a trellis that, from where we stood, partly shielded the back yard. "Hey," I shouted, craning to see the wagon, "they're moving in the rain! The furniture will get wet."

"Don't yell, Maggie." Mother pocketed the money and bent over the flowers. "What'll get wet?"

"Papa's bed. Look!" I yanked her hand away from the geranium. I'd never touched her like that before. "There! In the yard."

Mother peered around the trellis of honeysuckle vine. The loaded wagon was trundling through gray drops. "Frank's dresser too," she said low, creasing her forehead. "Can you stop them?"

"You were supposed to stop them." I ran down the steps. Slanting drops hit my face as I chased the wagon, a few yards ahead. The tall dresser mirror trembled with the rough turn of the wheels. "Wait!" I yelled. "It's raining."

Mitch twisted on the wagon seat; he wore overalls, no shirt, and the dark wet skin of his shoulders shone. "It ain't raining much," he called. "Can I go?"

"No, wait," I panted, catching up. Ahead, Ezra was swinging open the smokehouse door. They were half way. "Oh, go ahead. But hurry!" I stopped, mid-yard, and Mitch slowly plowed on. My white blouse was sticking to my skin, and drops were hitting Papa's tall walnut headboard. "Damn," I said, and made a fist. "Damnit to hell!" I didn't care if we never got moved. I didn't care if we just had to camp out in a field.

Cool rain washed my face. At least it wasn't freezing rain. The drops were becoming lighter, fewer. I took a breath down to my toes, then slouched back to the porch and Mother. She stood with a veined hand on a green rocker that was yet to be moved. No, I couldn't picture her sleeping in a field.

"They can wipe those pieces off," Mother said as I dragged up the steps. Her eyes behind her glasses seemed dim. "You dry off too," she said. "I'm going to see if I can find the black salve we smear on the chickens' legs for mites."

"Mother, we're moving," I said tersely. "Bird's getting the chickens." Pushing open the screen door, I added in a softer tone, "Just give the black salve to Bird."

In early afternoon the light rain let up, then started again, but not by much. Bird was in the kitchen boxing up pots and pans, and Mother was back in Josephine's Room. Mitch and Ezra were waiting to load the porch rockers. Our steps—Augusta's and mine—sounded hollow as we walked into Elizabeth's old room.

"The walls of Jericho are falling," said Augusta in a piping voice. "They're falling down." She stepped inside the dark closet and began heaping dresses, hangers, and all over her scrawny yellow-brown arm. I stood outside the door, waiting for whatever she couldn't hold. We were going to pile these clothes in the car, then later take them to the rented house in town.

Augusta twisted this way and that, shoving clothes and hangers, as if she were in a closet-clearing race. "Slow down. That's what you told me," I cautioned. "I don't want *you* falling down."

Not long ago she had fallen—passed out. Gave me a scare. We had rented a freezer locker at a new place in town to store vegetables, put up meat. The refrigerated room was large with stacks of lockers on top of each other, as in a bus station. Our locker was on the very top row, and I had to climb a ladder on wheels to reach it. Augusta was with me one day when I stopped by the freezer locker. She wanted to come in with me. The huge room felt extra cold. I was shaking by the time I found a ladder, rolled it to the right spot, and climbed up. Standing below, August hugged herself and talked about the place being a funny kind of smokehouse. As I handed down the second package, I saw her reel, then slide to the floor. The cold had gotten her. I ran for the manager. Augusta recovered quickly, and ever since then she loved to hear me describe what happened. "Tell 'bout how I fainted in the freezer locker," she would say. It was as if she'd had a starring role in a play. I'd tell the incident again.

In the closet Augusta was so tangled up with clothes, she seemed to have forgotten about the time she fell. She tossed Mother's brown sweater my way. "The walls of Jericho are coming down," she repeated.

"The walls of Jericho? That doesn't fit," I said, although it was true that something was surely coming to an end—you could hear it in our steps on the bare floor. I was glad to have Augusta's talk to fix my mind on. "Wasn't Jericho a bad place? God's people were outside wanting to get in. We're not bad people, Augusta, are we?"

"The walls of Jericho are falling," Augusta chirped again, ignoring my question, pitching clothes at me as though she were helping bring the walls down.

"Someone blew a trumpet that brought them down," I said. "Joshua! That's who."

"There's a Joshua Thomas that live on the hardroad." Augusta piled on the last dress. "We be passing his house when we ride in. I'm going to town with you."

I tiptoed and eyed the boxes of junk still on a shelf above Augusta's head. No telling what was inside—patterns, old gloves, buttons—my grandmother's? My stomach felt funny. But I came down off my toes, glad we didn't have to clear every last shelf today. Gil said to leave the corners for him. The walls of Jericho were almost down.

Augusta popped out of the closet, arms loaded, and we heard someone holler in the hall, "Bird's passed out." It was Mother. "Come quick!" she cried. "Her house is on fire!"

Augusta and I tossed the clothes on the bed and rushed down the hall, overtaking Mother.

Bird was sitting in the middle of the kitchen floor, holding the black stove-lid opener as if she'd been about to use it before she caved in. Her head lolled, but her eyes were opening. She was coming to. Ed Donaldson, back for a load of thrown-out kitchen stuff, was behind her, and he slipped his hands under her arms to pull her up. "I didn't mean to scare Miz Bird," he said, giving a high giggle. "I just said it looked like a fire up the road, might be her house. I didn't say it *war* her house."

"Lord Jesus, just like me in the freezer locker," said Augusta. "Take it easy, Conaway. Ain't no house burning. It's raining."

"There's a fire," mumbled Bird. She leaned on Ed's arm and mine.

"Look at the smoke!" said Mother, staring out the kitchen window. "See, over the pecan trees?"

I ran to the window, leaving Bird struggling to stand. "It's coming from the Acre all right," said Mother, hands on the sill. "Something's burning even in this weather."

I wished Mother wouldn't scare Bird, but she didn't realize what she was doing. "Bird, it's coming from around your house, all right," she added.

"Stop it, Mother! Bird's on the floor." I was mad. But Mother acted like she hadn't heard. "This rain isn't stopping it either," she said. "That's heavy smoke."

"Hush! We don't know what's burning."

"Burning in the rain!" Augusta said, looking out. "Walls of Jericho falling everywhere."

"Here comes Tug!" I cried. He was Bird's neighbor. "He'll tell us." Tug, in a bright red sweater, was hurrying over the stile near the pump house. Augusta ran out to meet him. Seeing him worried me. He'd bought the oak dining room table and would have been coming anyway to pick it up, but this was too quick.

Running back in, Augusta said, "Conaway, it's a house, but it ain't yours!"

"It's further down the road," said Tug, close behind Augusta. "The Jacksons', and they're all standing in the yard watching it burn in the rain." He stopped and stared at Bird with round eyes. Hand shaking, Bird laid the sooty lid-opener back on the stove. On the warmer was Bird's shiny pan, loaded with rice and ham to take home. Last food from that stove.

"My house ain't on fire," Bird whispered as though it were a secret. But her knees gave way again and she sank to the floor.

Seeing Bird sitting, I thought: well, now we can't leave. Bird helpless, the Jacksons standing in their yard, homeless. The two youngest used to come with Dollbaby to our playhouse.

Mother began talking about what we could send the Jacksons, not making much sense. The rest of us were propping Bird up. "Maybe I ought to go home," Bird said. "Burning in the rain!"

I helped Bird to her feet as Mother wandered aimlessly out to the porch. Not only Mother, but Bird, acting dopey.

However Bird recovered quickly. She didn't go home, but she sent word to the Jacksons that she'd bring some food. Their house hadn't burned down all the way, Tug found out. The fire had started when a child accidentally dumped live coals on some rags on the back porch; only the porch and the rear room burned.

Later I sat at the kitchen table by the window, my head resting on my hand. Outside the sky was a washed blue-gray. Mitch and Ezra were making the last run to the smokehouse. I was tired of trying to tell them when to wait and when to go. If it drizzled again, those rockers could just get good and soaked.

Bird and I talked about the rain—how we could still see a drop or two when we looked toward the opened door of the smokehouse. Then we were quiet. A wave of sadness slid over me. Mother was leaving a lot around this place—some things finished, some never even faced. No wonder she was addled.

Bird used a sooty poker to jiggle the remains of the stove fire. I could hear the muffled hits and the ashes sifting down to the pan below. A little dust rose. Bird bent over, gazing into the opening as I'd seen her do a million times, and wiggled the poker against the metal ribs.

"I want to leave this stove clean," said Bird. She picked up the tiny shovel and opened the bottom door. Slowly she piled ashes into an old lard bucket, dull-silver and dented on one side.

"Think we ought to take this bucket to town?" asked Bird. She was going to cook for us there, like always, except she wouldn't be coming back for the evening meal. She'd fix noon dinner only. We'd worked that out. Gil would pick her up in the morning and Mother would drive her home in the afternoon—six days a week instead of seven.

"No, we'll have an electric stove. You know."

"Good-bye bucket, then," said Bird, straightening. "I'll chunk it out with the ashes."

"Yes, you can chunk that old bucket," said Mother coming in from the back yard, two lilies in one hand. "You'll learn to cook on our new stove all right. But I want it to be gas, Maggie, not electric. Bird needs to see the little flame."

Mother was talking about new stoves! "Sure. A gas stove sounds good if they don't cost too much. Where'd you get the flowers?" The lilies looked orange and aggressive, as though they'd never droop their heads.

"From the garden, this early. Aren't they bright and perky? And I dug these up." She opened the other hand, showing three earth-covered sprouting bulbs. "These will transplant, I think. Tiger lilies are strong. I want to see some more bloom."

"Those opened-up ones must think it's spring," I said and smiled.

"They bloomed early 'cause we're leaving," said Bird. She gave a low chuckle, lifting the ashes-filled lard bucket.

"Bird, did you pack the baking tin for the cornsticks?" Mother asked, looking at the table loaded with boxes.

"Yes'um," Bird said and headed for the door.

"I think gas stoves cost about the same as electric ones, Mother," I said. I needed the little flame too.

After five, daylight beginning to fail, we climbed into the car—Augusta, Mother, and me. Bird had decided to go home, check on her house, see if any sparks drifted over. Augusta wanted to help unload and see the rented house. "Walls of Jericho done fallen," she said, getting in. We didn't linger. We drove out of the yard, left the dirt oval under the oaks that was either the end or the beginning of Spencer Road.

Augusta sat squeezed into the back seat with the clothes. Mother was in front, a pot of maidenhair fern at her feet and the two lilies in one hand, their stems wrapped in moss. The dug-up bulbs were tucked away somewhere.

"I'll put the lilies in water as soon as we get there," she said in a regular voice. "Later I'll plant the bulbs at our new house if I can find a special place."

"Sure you can," I said, smiling. I glanced sideways at the tiger lilies, at the orange petals, opened wide, like a hand. I didn't feel tired anymore or burdened with leaving. Mother was going to be all right. "After we move, you might even raise some to sell," I said, although I'd never thought of that before. "Gil will plant a garden in our new back yard. We can still raise string beans and peas."

Augusta leaned close to my ear. "Tell 'bout me fainting in the freezer locker."

"Well, you were standing below me, holding out your apron to put packages in," I said, talking sassy. "And when I passed down a package of corn, you began to sway. Like a tall pine in the wind."

"I had a swimming in my head. I did."

"Then your eyes rolled way, way back, and disappeared. You looked like a zombie."

Augusta clicked her tongue in wonder. Mother laughed, and I pressed on the gas so that the tires spun as we turned onto the hardroad, heading for town.

Epilogue ∿

The road is different now than it was back then. No longer would Bird feel at home walking its sandy ruts; neither would Augusta, who once clipped along near the ditch. If they could see Spencer Road now, they'd break their necks looking. Rather than gently angling off the pavement in front of St. Philip's Chapel, Bird's old church, the road takes a 90-degree turn off a four-lane highway, then cuts behind the church, no longer white and wooden but a cube of colorless cement.

Today, in a blue Toyota, I made the sharp turn and rolled onto the dirt. The ground had a clean, spongy feel, as though it had just been scraped. I hadn't driven down this road for months. In a weedy patch across from the church stood a tall, new sign—Days Inn, with a cartoon sun and an arrow pointing down the highway. The September sun glared brazenly on the sign. I slowed. That spot once held Sylvester Williams's unpainted house, his 4:00 A.M. rooster, his three brown dogs lazing in the swept yard. Sylvester's was easier on the eyes than the sign.

The road swung left and found its old path, its true course. My tires seemed to feel the change. I passed a ranch-style house, then a cedar one squatting in a plowed field that couldn't have been there long. Who lived there? More time must have passed than I thought since

I'd ridden along here. A small side road led off toward the cedar house, and on a green signpost, just like those in town, was the name—Donaldson Lane. Yes, I remembered the Donaldsons. They bought our old veneered bedroom suite. The father was Ed. He would be dead by now, but some of the grandchildren might actually be living in that very house, using the same bedroom suite.

Taking a hand from the wheel, I steadied the potted geranium in the passenger seat. I was taking it to Dollbaby—or Earlene as she was now called—who still lived in Bird's old house. I hadn't called beforehand to see if she would be at home. Buying the geranium had been an impulse. Earlier, in K-Mart, I'd seen a ton of them on display—pink blooms, red, white. We once had geraniums like those on our back porch. Mother grew them in green wooden boxes, positioned along the banister shelves so they could catch rainwater. The flowers seemed half on the porch and half in the yard, a good place to be. Mother liked the red ones best, and that's what I chose. Leaving the store, I had suddenly decided to take it to Earlene—probably because of yesterday's visit.

The Hunts, relatives from Alabama whom I rarely saw, had stopped by about four o'clock. I didn't mind the visit, and the fact that it was unannounced saved me from having to fix something special. I served them Sprite in frosted glasses, and we sat on my screened porch talking—Richard and Doris and I—while their twin boys kicked a soccer ball around the yard.

"We rode out to the old Spencer plantation yesterday," Richard said, pushing back in a rocking chair, glass held to his belt buckle. He was a round-shouldered, portly insurance salesman from Birmingham. Too much sitting at a desk, I thought.

"The Spencer plantation?" I said, although I had heard him perfectly. I could feel my smile grow thin.

"You know, Spencerwood." Richard gave me a direct stare.

"Spencerwood," I repeated, rubbing my glass, making circles in the moist film. When we lived there, no one called it that. Not much, anyway. "Spencerwood" was just home. Lately, other young cousins had taken to riding out to the place and acting as though they had discovered it.

Doris pushed back her sun-streaked hair. "The house is empty now, between owners. It's in fairly good shape. We walked around. I guess you've seen it, Maggie?"

Blood warmed my cheeks. Before answering, I looked toward the twins, now throwing a Frisbee. "I lived there for twenty-two years."

"You did?" Doris gave a toothy smile, then threw up a hand. "I should have known!"

"When was that?" Richard stopped rocking, his flecked eyes intent.

"Oh, not so long ago. At least it doesn't seem like it."

"You grew up there?" asked Richard, frowning.

What did he want? I thought. Proof? "Yes, and so did Gil and Elizabeth." I made a broad sweep with my hand toward the west, where the house was, as though taking full possession. "That was home until . . . we sold it."

Richard wrinkled his forehead as though still unconvinced. "Doris's grandfather grew up there, back before your time," he said. "Maybe your dad was around then."

I nodded.

Doris set her glass on an oak table that had come from the "out there"—that's how Gil referred to our old home. ("Have you ridden out there lately?" he'd ask, as though that dirt road led to another universe.) Doris said, "We told the boys their great-grandfather lived in that rambling white house a long time ago." She laughed, a good clear sound. "They asked if there used to be slaves around."

I took a long drink of Sprite. Bird's mother had been born in slavery, freed as a child. Richard and Doris would jump on that bit of southern lore, even though they might act as though it were terrible. But why tell them? They never knew Bird, and knew nothing about Josephine's Room, or the road-scraper grinding its way down our road, or April Fools' Day morning, Bird putting cotton in our oatmeal. They didn't know about driving home from church on a December night, snug in the car, turning off the hardroad and looking ahead for the orange glow of fire in the dark sky, and not seeing it, knowing our house was still safe. In spite of Papa's fears, it never burned.

"You know, some other cousins about your age were asking about the Spencer plantation not long ago." I glanced from Richard to Doris. "I guess folks like the idea of a plantation, but when we lived there. . . ." I stared through the tiny squares of the screen. "Well, it wasn't what you might think."

After they left, I didn't think of the old place again until I was leaving K-mart with the flower.

I parked the Toyota at the edge of the road, and holding the potted geranium, stepped over the shallow ditch. I climbed the three steps to Bird's old slanting porch—Earlene's porch now. Bird lay in Pall Bearers Cemetery off the clay road by the bullfrog pond; Augusta was only a few mounds away.

I knocked and waited. The door's blue paint was peeling, more off than on. Inside, no TV rumbled. I bent close to listen. I sensed the house as empty, still as an old photograph. During Bird's last illness, I sat by her bed in this very house on a summer Sunday afternoon. I wore a white pique dress, I remembered, and read aloud a psalm she'd asked for—number 121: "I will lift up mine eyes unto the hills, from whence cometh my help,"—while I fanned her with a cardboard church fan. She lay quiet, her knotted gray hair on the pillow, her dark cheeks sunk. The window was open and so was the door, and I could hear her two grandsons in the other room talking about the marches. It was the sixties. "They in Georgia now, coming to Al-benny. He's with them." I kept fanning, reading, and listening to them with half an ear. Bird just paid attention to the psalm; she didn't care what they said. But Augusta—if she'd lived longer, what an activist she'd have made. "Don't call me Negro; call me Colored!" she used to say. Her thin springy legs would have put her in the front lines of a march.

I knocked once more. Turning, I looked at the plants in cracked pots lined up on the edge of the porch. Three more—spidery ones—hung from above in white plastic bowls, the green tentacles tapering off, then bunching and cascading again, catching the light. Last time I visited, Earlene laughed and said she'd named those hanging plants for days of the week—Monday, Tuesday, Wednesday. Then, for some reason, she skipped to the bottom row and named one Thursday, and stopped there, giving the rest girls' names—Gertrude, Lena.

I stuffed my free hand in the pocket of my slacks. Should I leave the geranium, write a note, and tell Earlene I'd brought a plant that could be Friday? A red geranium like Mother used to grow. But I didn't have a pen in my bag, not even in the car. I could just leave the pot—place it next to Thursday with its tongue-shaped green shoots.

Setting it down, I bent close to the fuzzy leaves. Oh, that strong, geranium odor! It always reminded me of old dishwater, or weeds. "Pu-whee," I used to say to Mother, holding my nose, when she brought a cutting into the car and placed it next to me. This time I breathed in the smell.

I stood. Down the road, on the other side of Earlene's garden, was a trim yellow house, and in its yard a round-figured man dragged a rake across the swept ground. One of the Baileys, I thought. The Baileys had lived on the Acre forever, even after Tug began working in town. The raker looked familiar. It was Tug Bailey himself! Tug, twenty or so years older than me, still keeping up his yard. I could tell him about the geranium.

"You look so good, Miss Maggie, sure do," said Tug, laying the rake against the steps. He wiped his pale yellow palm on his pants and held out his hand.

"You look fine yourself," I said, shaking hands, "like a young, well, middle-aged man."

"I'm eighty-four," Tug said, as though living so long was a feat. We laughed, and Tug said he would be glad to tell Earlene about the flower. Her husband had taken her to the doctor; not much wrong, just the digestion.

Tug smiled, showing white, even teeth. "Yes'um, the geranium is Friday. I'll remember."

We kept talking, and in a minute I followed him inside to speak to his wife. Coralee sat in an armchair, pink afghan over her lap, black wig on her head. Faded eyes, but she remembered. "You the baby! Miss Maggie, you look fine." Tug turned down the TV, and they told about their children—a teacher, an accountant. We talked about Bird, the way she'd throw up her hand in greeting walking by their house on the way to ours; then about Gil and Elizabeth. I leaned back in my chair when they dropped the misses and misters. For a few minutes we were just Maggie and Elizabeth and Gil.

Tug led me back into the yard. "You're so nice and plump, Miss Maggie." Tug grinned, pausing near the steps. "We out here don't know why you don't get married again."

I wasn't plump at all—too bony, really—but he intended his comment as a compliment. "Not me, but Gil's boy, Raymond, is getting married soon," I said. "He's thirty-three, so it's time."

"Is that right? Gil's boy. Gil brought me some fish 'bout a month ago. Nice bream." Tug inhaled, warming to the subject of Gil, not his son. "Gil didn't hurry and get married hisself. Took him awhile, just like your daddy, Mr. Frank."

Nodding, I started toward my car in front of Earlene's. Tug walked beside me. "You know a long time, it was just your daddy up there at the home place with his mama and papa, all the brothers gone, gotten married. Seemed like a long time."

His comments slowed me. I hadn't heard this before, not exactly. I tried to picture Papa as a young man living in the house with his own parents, old people whose faces I'd never seen except in framed sepia-toned photographs that hung over the fireplace in the mile-long back bedroom. Papa, living in our house without Mother, without Gil and Elizabeth and me.

We passed Earlene's garden, weedy now with goldenrod along one side. "When Mr. Frank finally brought hisself home a bride, surprised even his own mama. Didn't nobody know! My auntie was working up there. I was a young boy, and they called us all to the house to meet her. She was tall and pretty, nice brown hair all piled up, and her looking this way and that, and your Papa, he was about to bust. Had on a fine suit."

I stopped and gazed down the road to where it curved out of sight. Never in all my years had I heard this. Why was it so hard to picture—Mother, in that house, a bride? Josephine's Room was probably a parlor then.

Finally, I said, "I guess Bird walked up there too."

"Oh, yes, Miss Maggie. That day we all went up the road to the house."

"You spoke to Mother?"

"Uh-huh. Your Papa was so proud! Looked just like Gil."

They always praise the men, I thought. Bird did too, always Gil.

I stepped toward the car, Tug beside me, telling how Mr. Frank gave him a piece of peppermint candy that day just before Tug left with his auntie. Tug ate the candy walking down the road to this very house, his own now. Tug swept with his hand. "You know we still call this Spencer Road."

Swinging open the car door, I smiled and said, "Our footprints are all around."

Instead of turning and heading back the way I came, I drove straight, past the Bridge Pond, the crossroads. I slowly took the curve.

The road didn't end or begin in the front yard anymore. The dirt surface swung around the shade trees and took off in a new direction, and further on, where the cowpen used to be, was the pitched roof of a new house. I bumped over to the old path, rolled onto the dirt oval, and stopped where we had always parked our car. The Ford, the maroon Chevy, and later the blue Studebaker. The Studebaker sat there the longest.

I climbed out, hungry to see. The house was still white but the pillars of the H-shaped porch were painted green. A bilious yellow-green! Maybe I should get right back in the car. I hadn't driven all the way up Spencer Road in so long, I didn't know about this change. I wouldn't have come today, except for Tug.

Still, the gray dirt felt familiar under my feet. No one else was in sight; everything quiet, except for the caw of a far-off crow. The oak branches cast the same shadows as back when Elizabeth and I played on the mossy roots. On the biggest tree, the old chain still grew out of the trunk. I touched the rusted links, then pulled on the chain with both hands. Bird once said it had been tied around the trunk when the tree was young, and used to tether horses. But the best time, I thought, was when we would hang on it and, hollering, swing from root to root. This time I took hold of the chain gingerly, leaned out, and hopped from one buckling root to another. I could still make it.

The japonica bush by the bay window of Josephine's Room looked stunted, the leaves brown-spotted, too pale a green. But at the corner of the house, the tea olive tree had grown wider, healthier; it was ready to bloom again next year. In the spring, when the windows were open, its delicate perfume would steal in. I would be sitting on the rug near Mother at the sewing machine. She might inhale and say, "Smell that tea olive, Maggie." I'd sniff and keep on cutting out the calendar pictures for the Sunday School scrapbooks that Mother made. Jesus, the Last Supper.

I stopped on the west side of the house, near the long windows of Josephine's Room. On the inside, the panes were covered with cardboard. In a way, that was good. I didn't want to see in.

Overhead, the sun was at two o'clock, and I felt its heat, not too oppressive today. In late afternoon, I remembered, the light on this side of the house was golden, drifting in the long windows, across the ironing board, touching the sewing machine and my mother's hands. Her strong fingers, no rings, feeding cloth under the galloping silver needle. When had she quit wearing her wedding ring? I wondered. She had one, I knew; I kept the gold band in a lacquer box at home. But I never saw her wear it. Did she just take it off one day and never put it back on?

I leaned against the white boards, liking their warmth, soaking it in. Back when this room was a parlor, a patterned burgundy rug probably filled the center, and a marble-top table and a sofa hugged one side. I could picture it, but not Mother and Papa in their thirties, standing in the center, newly married. Strange, Tug bringing up that special day, a decade before I was born—recounting it as if it were last year. Yet I remembered the other days that seemed more recent—Gil hunting in the woods, Elizabeth driving the Studebaker to town. And Gwen, trying to roll a log in the back yard in the shade of the old trees. Falling off, and later, that other fall. Gwen, fourteen forever.

Our time was as clear to me as a crystal glass, its fine cuts sparkling. Still, when Papa was a boy, he played in the same yard. Uncle Charlie once talked about climbing the big tree, the one that fell. All the brothers, he said, would crawl way out on its long branches until their mother called them in.

Many pasts existed, and I knew I didn't own them all. I surely didn't own the future. The next time a cousin told me about riding down Spencer Road, maybe I'd talk longer. I might even tell Richard and Doris how Bird, on the way to our house, would cut across the oak grove, and how we'd run to meet her. How Gus came for her at dark, how he'd climb over the wooden stile, a railroad lantern swinging in his hand.

Back in the Toyota, I drove quickly up the dirt road, passing Tug, still raking in the yard. I threw up my hand in Bird's old way. Beyond the church, I made the sharp turn onto the paved highway and stepped hard on the gas pedal. That night, I would go out, maybe visit Elizabeth or Gil.

〰 *Spencer Road* was designed and typeset on an Apple computer using PageMaker software. The text is set in Goudy Old Style, with display type set in Caslon Antique. This book was designed and composed by Kay Jursik, and was printed and bound at Thomson-Shore, Inc. The recycled paper used in this book is designed for an effective life of at least three hundred years.